MY YEAR OF READING WELSHLY

MY YEAR OF
READING WELSHLY

ALEX JOHNSON

2025

www.uwp.co.uk

British Library Cataloguing-in-Publication Data
A catalogue record for this book is available from
the British Library.

ISBN: 978-1-915279-78-1
The right of Alex Johnson to be identified as author of this work has been asserted in accordance with sections 77 and 79 of the Copyright, Designs and Patents Act 1988.

For GPSR enquiries please contact: Easy Access System Europe Oü, 16879218. Mustamäe tee 50, 10621, Tallinn, Estonia. gpsr.requests@easproject.com

Typeset by Agnes Graves
Cover design by Andy Ward
Printed and bound in Great Britain by CPI Group (UK) Ltd, Croydon, CR0 4YY
The publisher acknowledges the financial support of the Books Council of Wales

DEDICATION

To Mum and Dad,
Wilma, Thomas, Edward and Robert

CONTENTS

INTRODUCTION
Trying to solve
some kind of problem

So, what shall I read next?

Like you, I've asked myself that question on a regular basis for decades. Since I finished *Roderick the Red* in the *Griffin Pirate Stories* at infant school, I've hopscotched via the Rev. W. Awdry's *Railway Series*, to characters like Noggin the Nog, Tintin, Jennings and Darbishire and the Moomins, to Tolkien, to *The Eagle of the Ninth*, then *Vanity Fair* (yep, bit of a jump there – but that's what happens when you're the son of librarians) and Melissa Bank right up to my present-day mishmash which features the likes of C. J. Sansom, Mary Beard and Alice Oswald.

And while I enjoy reading, there's something very enjoyable in the thrill of the chase of a good read: the search for inspiration, the lucky find (or sometimes the unlucky find), the deliberating and then the pleasure of plumping for something promising. But how do you actually choose from the vast tables of colourful pristine goodies in the bookshop or the roomfuls of books in the library?

How I choose what to read next is pretty unsystematic. Rather like the invisible chain Scrooge is unwittingly forging for himself piece by piece in *A Christmas Carol*, but hopefully in a rather less disagreeable way, like many readers, I build up physical and mental piles of books I intend to dive into. I take advice from friends who read a lot – thank you, in particular, Emma and Judith – as well as from my wife who is always spot on with suggestions. In fact, there are few occasions when book recommendations don't come up in conversation. I play snooker every Wednesday with a group of friends and some years ago we were told off in no uncertain terms by players on a neighbouring table for allowing our discussions about whether *Tom Jones* was a suitable book club choice to become overly heated. I read book reviews in the media (mostly *The Guardian*, *Observer* and *The Sunday Times* newspapers, and *Literary Review* and *Slightly Foxed* magazines). I listen to the occasional literary podcast (mostly *Backlisted*), and regularly pop into my local bookshop, Books on the Hill in St Albans, which always serves up an interesting selection on its front table. It is also the only shop in town where they know my name. If you discount a couple of the pubs. And the snooker club.

This book will offer up a selection of my personal recommendations about what *you* might want to have a go at after you've finished your current read. There's a pretty hefty clue in the title of this book about what I'll be suggesting but, before I properly introduce my choices, let's think about ways and means of approaching the challenge.

Books are being published in greater numbers than ever before, but the challenge facing readers in making their next choice is nothing new. One way to beat through the literary bracken is to implement a reading programme to provide some helpful navigation. One of the earliest examples of this kind of self-improvement was the work of nineteenth-century MP Sir John Lubbock who, in addition to introducing the groundbreaking 1871 Bank Holidays Act, was principal of the Working Men's College in London, where he gave a speech in 1886 in which he put together arguably the first books listicle.

'I drew up the list,' he said, 'not as that of the hundred best books, but, which is very different, of those which on the whole are perhaps best worth reading.' This hundred 'best-but-not-best' list of titles, all from authors who were at the time already dead, was then published and circulated widely, encouraging people to have a crack at centuries of literature including *The Meditations* of Marcus Aurelius, the writings of Epictetus, Thomas à Kempis's *Imitation of Christ*, portions of *The Koran*, the entire works of Shakespeare and Molière along with Austen's *Pride and Prejudice* and Dickens's *David Copperfield* offered as lighter reads.

While Lubbock's strategy is commendably worthy, it's too much like a funless university reading list for my liking. It's a bit too wholemeal when I'd prefer something a little more country grain. Yet there is something appealing about a proper plan for your reading. For the last decade or so my largely scattergun approach has had a loose structure: I read a work of fiction, followed by something non-fiction and then a poetry collection on a continually revolving basis. Within that I also make a conscious effort to pick women writers, mix up recently published titles with established classics, and leaven it all with collections of cartoons, photobooks, back copies of *Tiger and Scorcher* annuals and the occasional graphic novel. At Christmas I always reread *The Box of Delights*, *A Christmas Carol* and Raymond Briggs's *Father Christmas*.

There are, of course, gaping holes in my reading history, but the problem is knowing which ones should I plug. It's as hard to choose what to read next as it is to choose a perfectly ripe melon, and recommendations pile in significantly faster than I can read. Should this year be, finally, the year I read Proust? Is it time to try reading all the past Booker Prize winners? Maybe it's time to try the *Miss Read* books from the very start? Or, as one of the most bookish of all my friends is attempting, all the books in Jane Austen's personal library? Perhaps George Macdonald Fraser's *Flashman* series in chronological order? And while I dither, my living space starts to more closely embody the Japanese term *tsundoku*: the habit of accumulating books but leaving a wincingly high number of them unread in piles or untouched on bookshelves.

There's no shortage of books by other readers who have asked themselves the same question 'What should I read next?' and then written their own book about the experience thereby adding to the growing number of books of book lists. The most straightforward approach is the 'Great Books' approach. Andy Miller rounded up fifty titles in his excellent 2014 personal literary odyssey, *The Year of Reading Dangerously*. What he described as his 'List of Betterment' was based on a simple desire to finally tackle head on the classics that he – and, let's be brutally honest, many others of us – have never finished or, indeed, even started. Similarly, for his book *The Whole Five Feet*, published half a dozen years earlier, Christopher Beha read all fifty-one volumes of *The Harvard Classics*: a roll call of books assembled by former Harvard president Charles William Eliot. The complete collection, when lined up, would fill a shelf measuring five feet. Eliot believed reading this collection was 'a means of obtaining such a knowledge of ancient and modern literature as seems essential to the twentieth-century idea of a cultivated man.'

The same year as Miller, Phyllis Rose's *The Shelf: Adventures in Extreme Reading* took a rather more random bookish plunge when she decided to narrow her reading down to a few shelves in the New York Society Library, choosing on a whim the shelves labelled LEQ to LES. She felt that this would be a truly unique selection. In *Howards End Is on the Landing: A Year of Reading From Home*, Susan Hill matched Rose's cheap budget of zero but stayed closer to home. In fact, she stayed *at* home and spent a year rereading what she already had on her bookshelves rather than buying anything new. Alberto Manguel kept the number of books on his list much, much lower by simply rereading a dozen of his favourites when he wrote *A Reading Diary: A Year of Favourite Books*. Then there are the single author specialists, such as *Out of Sheer Rage: Wresting With D. H. Lawrence* by Geoff Dyer, *My Life in Middlemarch* by Rebecca Mead, and *My Salinger Year* by Joanna Rakoff, who cover the collected works of one writer.

As well as asking myself *what* to read next, I ask *why* I want to read it. Beha's book is subtitled *What the Great Books Taught Me About Life, Death and Pretty Much Everything Else*. That feels slightly on the ambitious side. While reading offers the chance to learn about something I know almost nothing about, the problem is that this amounts to a monstrous list of ignorance about almost everything: flowers, Antarctica, quantum physics, sharks, Gilbert and Sullivan operas and rice. Again, at the very genuine risk of sounding like a loafer, I think the idea of filling in all my knowledge gaps is too aspirational.

So, how about something I know a bit about and that I'm interested in pursuing a bit further? My parents have a complete collection of every *King Penguin* title published by Penguin from the late forties onwards. With titles ranging from *Magic Books from Mexico* to *Some British Beetles*, these would certainly fill my knowledge tanks. Another plus point is that they are all very short and are also full of illustrations. Two of my friends at the snooker club have read pretty much all of Dickens and I sometimes feel I'd like to contribute more to the occasional conversations we have about his work. The downside there is that I'm not that keen on Dickens, so the idea of ploughing through a dozen novels and god knows how many short stories is not that appealing – even though *The Lazy Tour of Two Idle Apprentices* he wrote with Wilkie Collins sounds like just the thing. Also, I don't want this to be a competitive read-off contest. I just want to have a few rules to help me along because, as Monica says in *Friends*, 'Rules are good. Rules help control the fun.'

What I'm looking for is something with which I'm currently on neighbourly nodding terms but would be happy to get to know a little better – nothing too serious, just something I'd be happy to go out for a pint with, maybe even to the cinema. While I was at the 'throwing ideas around like confetti' stage, a friend kindly pointed me in the direction of the American economist and blogger Tyler Cowen, who is a voracious reader and regularly writes on the subject. His advice that 'the best reading is focused reading, when you're trying to solve some kind of problem' was useful. In my case, the problem was identifying a suitable literary challenge. His suggestion that you read topics you know nothing about was also useful in my decision-making.

In the spirit of bookish list creation, I started to make a new one of potential ideas and among the many I discounted were:

- biographies of every English monarch in chronological order (the downside being a strong possibility of not making it past Cnut)
- all the books on my shelves which I've never read (the major downside being that there are just too many)
- the *Sharpe* novels by Bernard Cromwell (there's a decent number, but do I want to spend that much time in the Napoleonic wars?)
- the *Falco* Ancient Roman detective novels by Lindsey Davis (again, do I want to spend that much time in 69 AD–89 AD and do you include the sequels about his daughter?)
- a whole year of just reading poetry (no downside but... well, that's a *lot* of poetry)
- all the books on David Bowie's list of one hundred favourite reads (upside: any list that includes the *Beano* has considerable appeal).

I won't go on because, unless you've got this far without looking at the cover of this book – in which case congratulations on remarkable, if somewhat bewildering, patience – the idea that made it over the line was, of course, Wales. It's perhaps a slightly surprising choice for someone who isn't Welsh, can't speak the language, and has never lived in Wales but bear with me.

I was born in the Welsh Marches, and I grew up in Wellington, a small market town in Shropshire near Shrewsbury, where I lived until I was thirteen. Although only one or two of the pupils at my primary school were Welsh, our teacher in my final year was Dai Morris, a man who, learning that our music teacher Mrs Duncalf had been teaching the choir 'Bread of Heaven' so that we could sing it in assembly the following day, rather subversively tried to teach me the lyrics in Welsh so at least one person could give it some '*Cwm Rhondda*'.

Although the school was not located in Wales, it always seemed to be glancing happily westwards towards it. Our school choirs sang at the *eisteddfodau* in Llangollen and at other choral competitions in Welsh towns. We went on school trips to Welsh seaside. I remember doggedly collecting examples of bladderwrack on the beach at Borth despite driving horizontal rain. For our school trip at the end of year six, we went camping in Harlech. And while, as far as I know, there isn't a drop of Welsh blood in my body, my parents met at university in Bangor in the 1960s when there were still only about 500 students in the entire year and Welsh nationalism was on the rise. One student in their tutor group would only answer questions addressed to her in Welsh, and another wrote essays on English imperialism in Welsh, irrespective of the question set (she only lasted a term). While it seems trivial, the final clincher was that a good friend of mine whom I meet up with regularly is also Welsh, and his enthusiasm for his country is pleasantly infectious. It's hard *not* to find Wales and its culture appealing – it proudly boasts a beautiful landscape, a rich and long sporting and musical history (the crowd's rendition of the National Anthem at fixtures is immensely moving), a distinctive culture, and an intriguing industrial heritage. There is so much to explore in and about Wales and so much *I* have never explored. So, it was to Wales that I turned for my reading inspiration.

The next step was to decide what and how many books to read. This was difficult since I was dealing with unknown unknowns – or perhaps known unknowns – as I was making a list of books that I had largely never heard of before by writers who were largely unfamiliar to me. When I asked friends for suggestions, most answers didn't get me much beyond Dylan Thomas or the occasional 'wasn't Jan Morris Welsh?' or 'didn't Roald Dahl live in Wales?'. Some people half-remembered poets, some of whom shared surnames. Charlotte Church got a couple of namechecks, as did Griff Rhys Jones, Russell T Davies and 'the bloke who wrote Ivor the Engine'. I began with a pretty short list of recommended titles that included *I Bought a Mountain, How Green Was My Valley*, the *Mabinogion* and *Under Milk Wood*, and then tailed off sharply. A few people, all of them either Welsh or academics and often both, came up with hugely impressive lists of writers that ran from Taliesin (an entirely new name to me) to Joe Dunthorne (I smiled smugly to myself because I had actually read him, but without realising he is Welsh).

I took all of these suggestions on board, sniffed around the internet for more ideas, asked more friends, took a look at what I already had on the shelves, and came up with a selection. My criteria were that the books would:

* have been published in the last hundred years, from 1924 to 2024, to allow me to get some kind of idea of how things have changed (this meant no *Mabinogion*, which is a book so vast and complex that it would require a whole separate book and somebody more expert than me to do it justice anyway).
* only be books written in English or translated into it because my Welsh is far too poor to read anything in the original.
* include fiction (adult, children or YA), travel and poetry, but no history because what I wanted was a kind of feel for the country and how it has been reflected in its literature over the last century rather than a detailed official account, however informative that might be.

In terms of numbers, Alberto Manguel's idea of one book a month for a year felt, in the nicest possible way, a bit slack (not that I'm opposed to being a bit slack – I've written regularly for *The Idler* magazine for the last decade and missed deadlines equally regularly). On the other hand, it would probably take me three years to emulate Ann Morgan's feat of reading a book from every independent country on the planet (196 in total) for her *Reading the World: Confessions of a Literary Explorer.* And as for Nina Sankovitch's diet of a book a day for twelve months for her *Tolstoy and the Purple Chair: My Year of Magical Reading*... Well, I'll hit those numbers when they next ask me to be a Booker Prize judge and not before.

So, on the basis of all things in moderation, fifty-two books in a year seemed an achievable number, especially as I read around that number a year usually. I picked about forty-five, which I figured would leave me some wriggle room for adding ones in as I went along if I enjoyed a particular author or received more recommendations as more people found out about what I was doing. I wanted to be flexible. To reflect on what Barbossa says about the Pirate Code in *Pirates of the Caribbean*: I just needed to lay down more of what you'd call guidelines than actual rules. Writing this book was going to be enjoyable, not a literary press gang.

I keep a list of everything I read every year but I don't write anything else about them other than put an asterisk by the ones I really enjoyed so, when I look back, I have no idea why. On a purely selfish basis, I wanted this book to be more of a diary for myself of my year of reading Welshly, and so wrote up my thoughts as soon as I'd finished each book and it was still fresh in my mind. There's only one book in this collection which I gave a good kicking to and it will be obvious when you get to it. At the end of each section, I've also included a snap summary of thoughts about why the book matters, why I think you should read it or why you might want to give it a miss, and what I learned about Wales from it, which I hope helps give you more ammunition in deciding whether it is for you. There's a full bibliography at the end of the book that you could use as a handy checklist.

In life generally, I'm all for staying securely within my happy place, but when it comes to reading, nearly all of us have a tendency to play it a bit too safe in terms of choosing authors and books. I'm certainly guilty of this myself. Having completed the book, I found myself amazed at the breadth and talent of Welsh writers, both ancient and modern, and – while Dylan Thomas and Ivor the Engine are both smashing (well, I think so) – there is so much more to discover.

Writing this book has been a lot of fun for me, and I think it could be very enjoyable for you, too, however much or little you know about Wales and the books that have sprung from it. I'm clearly not an expert in Welsh literature, but I do hope some of the enthusiasm I've found during my private reading odyssey might rub off on you and that you will want to have a go at some of the titles I've included, especially the ones you've never heard of. How many of them you choose to crack the spines of (or consume via audio) is naturally up to you. You could read all fifty-two, what we could fairly describe as the gold (*aur* in Welsh) level. Don't feel though that you have to consume the lot within a twelve-month period. This is pretty hardcore. I'll be honest, I found fifty-two at the pace of one a week a bit of a stretch and needed a book breather about halfway through, but if you're looking for a challenge then by all means go ultimate. But you may choose to spread them out a bit or mix them up with other reading to vary your literary diet.

Those aiming for the silver or *arian* level can happily halve the workload and have a go at twenty-six. A book a fortnight is still a big ask but it's not quite so intimidating or relentless in pace, and consequently you're more likely to finish it. It also gives you significant wriggle room to pick and choose whatever takes your fancy from the list and use it as a springboard to follow your own interests. My advice would still be to mix it up a bit rather than only select, say, novels on the basis that, with apologies to the eighteenth-century poet William Cowper, variety is the spice of reading, that gives it all its flavour.

For a dozen, I think you should proudly award yourself a bronze, or *efydd* level. This number could also work well if you fancy setting up a Reading Welshly monthly book group with like-minded folk who want to explore the books together, with or without a side helping of wine and nibbles. If that is the case then, to help get the party started, I've included some possible questions for each title at the back of the book to stimulate conversation or maybe angry debate.

If only one book feels like a good fit for you, then that's also great. I don't know what to call this level but I'd say it still very much counts as a win. Reading should be a pleasure, not a to-do list.

Whichever route you take – or even if you decide, having read this book, not to read a single one of the books I explore – I'd genuinely love to hear from you about what you thought both of this book and the books of Welsh interest that you go on to read. (I'm quite easy to find on social media so please do @ me).

Now, enough about the challenges of choosing a worthy read. Let's head back to 1925.

BOOK 1

ANGELS IN ANGUISH

◆

The Battle to the Weak
by Hilda Vaughan
(1925)

Entirely by chance, my first book choice opens, appropriately, with a Welsh creation story.

> For an hour after sunrise, a shepherd who stood upon the summit of the Garth might have believed himself returned to the first days of creation ... Now the world was without form and void; the valley beneath and the hills beyond were alike hidden.

This feels like a propitious start.

With some books, I wonder just how their author pitched them to an agent. Jim Butcher described his *Codex Alera* fantasy series as 'Pokémon meets lost Roman legion', while Erin Beaty said in an interview that she pitched her young adult novel *The Traitor's Kiss* as '*Jane Eyre* meets *Mulan*'. I've not read either of them but the pitches alone have me interested. I've also seen somebody in an online forum suggesting that *Watership Down* is *Peter Rabbit* meets Xenophon's *Anabasis,* a pitch that would surely have intrigued any publisher worth their salt at a pitch meeting.

I don't know how Hilda Vaughan (1892–1985) pitched this book to her publishers but, for me, it's very definitely *Romeo and*

Juliet set in Radnorshire (mid-Wales, next to Shropshire – I had to look it up on a map). The premise is, essentially, a mischievous prank by a neighbour sets up a decades-long feud between the Lloyd and Bevan families in a small rural community. It also evokes something of a Welsh ethnic hostility since chapel-going, teetotaller Elias Lloyd is 'a type still to be found among the Celtic peoples of Wales... his yellowish complexion suggested kinship with the Portuguese' while church-going, heavy drinker John Bevan is red-haired.

Their teenage offspring Esther Bevan and Rhys Lloyd fall in love despite their families' feud, but the fierce opposition from their parents and siblings eventually leads to Rhys getting the hump and upping sticks to Canada. Esther has the additional heartache of dealing with her increasingly drunken father, who makes home life extremely unpleasant. Although rural lifestyles are often presented in the novel as preferable, especially morally, to urban ones, there's no sugarcoating of how much work is involved in working the land, especially for women whose life options are severely limited. Without dishing up any spoilers, there's no grand 'happy ever after' ending (indeed, some of the characters have distinctly rotten endings). A contemporary reviewer in the *Western Mail* suggested it was 'Wales depicted truly at last'.

Some books written a century ago feel remarkably up-to-date. I'd stick the comic misadventures of Mr Pooter in *The Diary of a Nobody* (1892) by George and Weedon Grossmith in that category, as I would Jerome K. Jerome's *Three Men in a Boat (To Say Nothing of the Dog)* (1889). *The Battle to the Weak*, however, does not make it in. It's nicely written and hums along well, but it does feel a little creaky at times and even teeters on the cliff edge of melodrama. Esther's dad, John Bevan, often feels like one of those pantomime-ish baddies from silent movies twirling their moustache and begging to be booed.

This was Vaughan's first novel so I don't want to be too hard, especially as she's showcasing the country at an important crossroads when new ideas were seen as a threat. Esther's traditional religious values collide with the nonconformist Lloyds and Rhys's embrace of scientific Social Darwinism and his goal of reforming Wales. He has an unfortunate tendency to mansplain as well as an inclination to romanticise a Welsh 'golden age' involving lots of harps and poetry. 'The problem of civilisation, it seems to me,' he says while observing animals at an agricultural show, 'is how to maintain competition between races and individuals whilst eliminating its present cruelty.' Esther is open to discussion but is much less sure than Rhys that he is entirely right. Indeed, the title and thrust of the book (a nod to the passage in 'Ecclesiastes': 'the race is not to the swift, nor the battle to the strong') indicates Vaughan's thoughts about the concept of the survival of the fittest.

My 2010 Library of Wales edition published by Parthian has an enigmatic painting by Welsh artist Clive Hicks-Jenkins on the cover, 'The Angels in their Anguish'. The painting is based on Piero della Francesca's '*Madonna del Parto*' ('Our Lady of the Partition'), a painting of the pregnant Virgin Mary. In the introduction to the book, novelist Fflur Dafydd argues that 'The whole range of woman's experience is to be seen in this rich tapestry of a novel.'

Although that might be pushing it a bit, there certainly is a decent number of strong female characters battling largely insensitive men. Esther's straitlaced upbringing is in contrast to her aunt Polly's approach to life. 'And why shouldn't an 'oman be havin' her fancy same as a man?' she asks when talking about sexual permissiveness, which feels like a very modern approach. Her sister also forcefully points out that 'Allus takin' the easy jobs for theirselves the boys is ... There's Father today, ridin' off to Llangantyn as soon as he's had his breakfast – like a king just, after me puttin' a polish on his boots – and poor Mother walkin' all the way to town when she's done her morning's work, carryin' two great old baskets full o' butter and eggs.' As the narrator points out, 'Incessant drudgery, poor health, poorer spirits and overmuch childbearing had reduced Annie Bevan [John's wife] to a wraith.' Esther herself is stoically angelic, calm under pressure, and has a strong sense of duty, though an unkind commentator might suggest that she makes herself a bit of a martyr.

As with many of the writers on my Welshly list, I'd never heard of Vaughan before I picked up her book. She was born in Llanfair-ym-Muallt (Builth Wells), just south of Radnorshire, where she set her story. She wrote nine more novels (in English) and her last in 1954. During the First World War, she served in the Women's Land Army in her native Breconshire and Radnorshire where she met many women on local farms. Although she became part of London's literary scene and was on the fringe of the Bloomsbury set in London (George Bernard Shaw professed himself 'dazzled' by her beauty), she preferred to return to Wales for several months of the year to write her books.

The Battle to the Weak was originally published by W. Heinemann in 1925 and received very positive reviews. Over her lifetime, reviewers both from the Welsh press and further afield compared Vaughan to George Eliot and suggested that she was doing for Radnorshire what the Brontës had done for Yorkshire. Or as the *West Sussex Gazette* pitched it: '*Far from the Madding Crowd* in the depths of the Welsh countryside'.

Why this book matters... it depicts the arrival of a new way of thinking in Wales.

Read it because... the female characters drive the action.

Give it a miss if... you find Victorian novels a bit creaky.

What I discovered about Wales... rural life can be very limiting.

BOOK 2

A QUESTION OF MARKETING

◆

In Parenthesis
by David Jones
(1937)

The beauty of a reading scheme like this is that it throws up finds that you've not only never heard of but, in all likelihood, you would never have otherwise picked up. I'm slightly embarrassed to say that *In Parenthesis* (or the strangely broken *In Paren-thesis* as the cover of my 1975 Faber reprint presents it) by David Jones falls into this category for me. Although I like to think I've read a decent amount of poetry, I'd never heard of either the poet or the title of the book, which gives no immediate indication about its contents. The publisher's more recent edition at least has an arresting cover – a drawing of a desolate and war-torn battlefield with soldiers stuck in the mud alongside a horse and a piece of heavy artillery. My copy has the old-fashioned design, which looks worthy but dull.

I suspect I am not alone in never having heard of David Jones. Asked to name First World War poets, I'd bet the general public would stick Wilfred Owen and Siegfried Sassoon at the top of the list, with Rupert Brooke on a rung just behind them. Perhaps a couple of others like Ivor Gurney and Edward Thomas might get a namecheck. David Jones (1895–1974) would not bother the scorers. Born and brought up in England, his father was Welsh, and Jones regarded himself as Welsh, too, although he never lived in the country. The longest he spent in Wales was during a series of visits in the late 1920s.

But, in our ignorance of David Jones's work, I and the wider general public have been missing out. *In Parenthesis* is quite astonishing – a literary stew that tasted to me of Alan Garner's *Treacle Walker* and T. S. Eliot's *The Waste Land* with the musical resonance of Benjamin Britten's 'War Requiem'. It stirs together the essence of Garner's eccentric final novel, Eliot's highly allusive poem, and Britten's composition, which combines Wilfred Owen's war poetry with Latin liturgy. If you were intrigued by Max Porter's prose poem approach in his novella *Grief Is the Thing With Feathers*, you will definitely by intrigued by *In Parenthesis*.

The book is divided into seven parts with an explanatory preface that is essential reading before you start. If you skip it, you'll be constantly scratching your head as you work through the main text. The book is loosely based on Jones's own experience of fighting at Mametz Wood during the Battle of the Somme. It begins in December 1915 with his main character, John Ball, an infantryman in the Royal Welch Fusiliers, made up mostly of Welsh and cockney soldiers, which offers the reader dialogue in both English and Welsh with plenty of military language.

The battalion travel from England towards the front and experience some pretty ghastly fighting, more of the common and garden realistic variety that really hits home rather than the kind that might be seen in a spectacular Hollywood set piece. It's not a clichéd 'plucky Tommy Atkins fights off The Bosch' story, but more Jones's observation that the natural world is being replaced by comprehensive, mechanised slaughter, with exactly the amount of laughs you'd expect in such a situation. At the end, Ball is seriously wounded and has visions of tourists visiting the battlefield. Jones himself was wounded after serving for 117 weeks at the front, more than any other First World War British poet.

W. H. Auden described *In Parenthesis* as 'the greatest book about the First World War'. Actor Richard Burton was said to have had a copy on his bedside table. So why don't we know it better? Perhaps it's a question of marketing because the great and the good of the literary world have certainly given *In Parenthesis* high praise over the last ninety years since it was published. But perhaps it is simply because it is not an easy read. Poetry is not something to speed read. It requires thought and consideration, and Jones's work is absolutely no exception.

There's another challenge for the reader. There are plenty of references to everything in the poem from foundational Welsh texts like the *Mabinogion* and *Y Gododdin* to Lewis Carroll, the Bible, and Arthurian legends – a reflection of his breadth of reading rather than the inclusions of an intellectual show-off. Jones was very keen that the poem should be understood so reached out an illuminating hand by adding voluminous explanatory footnotes (technically endnotes, since they're all gathered together at the end of the book rather than the bottom of each page).

I'm not against footnotes or endnotes.[1] The ones in the *Flashman* series by George MacDonald Fraser add a valuable historical dimension to the antihero's misadventures, and those in Garrison Keillor's *Lake Wobegon Days* and Nicholson Baker's *The Mezzanine* enhanced my enjoyment. Further back, anybody

1 For more on footnotes, see *The Footnote: A Curious History* by Anthony Grafton (Faber/Harvard University Press, 1997), who describes them memorably as 'anthills swarming with otherwise unseen learning'. Also chapters in *Invisible Forms: A Guide to Literary Curiosities* by Kevin Jackson (Macmillan, 1999), and *Book Parts*, edited by Dennis Duncan and Adam Smyth (Oxford University Press, 2019).

who's toyed with Gibbon's *Decline and Fall of the Roman Empire* will give thanks for the light touches his mountains of footnotes give the work. And I'm not sure I don't actually prefer the footnotes in Terry Pratchett's *Discworld* series to the main text.

But the problem with *In Parenthesis* is that the footnotes themselves run to thirty pages in my edition, well over 10 per cent of the entire book, so it means a lot of to-ing and fro-ing. As Noël Coward put it, 'Having to read footnotes resembles having to go downstairs to answer the door while in the midst of making love.' Just to be clear, that's not how I read *In Parenthesis*, but the point still stands.

Moreover, for a lot of readers, the footnotes are going to need even more concentration because they, in turn, make reference to other texts, some of which are not especially well known. One endnote in part four is even sub-divided into separate sections marked A–N. This detail and complexity is not necessarily a problem, but it does slow things down even more. T. S. Eliot argues that this is not a bad thing. He suggests in his introduction to the first edition of *In Parenthesis* that this is not only a work of genius, but also a book that really does require rereading. He claims that we need to be 'excited by the text' first and then go back to it to understand it. He's certainly right about that. I enjoyed it, but on my first read I enjoyed the atmosphere the writing created for me rather than focusing on understanding what was going on a lot of the time. In a way, the extensive endnotes feel like having the iconography of a renaissance painting explained – while you can enjoy the art without the added information, it's much clearer what the artist is trying to achieve once you've been enlightened. Interestingly, Jones was also a remarkably good painter and engraver and worked particularly hard on *In Parenthesis* at a time when he was recovering from a nervous breakdown and taking a break from art on his doctor's orders. It does have a very visual, sensory feel to it and, indeed, began as a series of drawings with short pieces of accompanying text.

Why this book matters... it's a genuine one-of-a-kind reading experience.

Read it because... you want war poetry with a difference.

Give it a miss if... you don't like looking up references.

What I discovered about Wales... there are Welsh war poets.

BOOK 3

O, THERE IS LOVELY
TO FEEL A BOOK

◆

How Green Was My Valley
by *Richard Llewellyn*
(1939)

Even if you haven't read it, there's a decent chance you've seen the hugely successful black-and-white 1941 film adaptation of the book *How Green Was My Valley*, which stars a young Maureen O'Hara and an even younger Roddy McDowall. The film beat *Citizen Kane* and *The Maltese Falcon* to win the Best Picture Oscar. 'They knew the surging ecstasy of breathtaking love,' says the trailer dramatically, which is quite a contrast to scriptwriter Philip Dunne's view of the novel, which he described, I think harshly, as 'turgid'.

While the idea of this reading programme is very much to look beyond tired pigeon-holing and explore the depths of Welsh literature, *How Green Was My Valley* offers pretty much a full bingo card of Welsh clichés. Choirs – tick. Rugby – tick. Mining – tick. Valleys – tick. Daffodils – tick. Sheep – tick. A chapel – tick. A character called Ivor – tick. The book and film together are arguably responsible for establishing many of the stereotypes associated with the country. *How Green Was My Valley* sold 176,000 copies in the United States in 1940 *before the movie was released*, which was more than John Steinbeck's

21

The Grapes of Wrath, which was also published in 1939. But stereotypes aside, I also found it a tremendous read.

Like *The Battle to the Weak*, it's a story of everyday Victorian country folk. But although written only fourteen years later than Vaughan's novel, it feels significantly more modern. In fact, what it feels like to me is a forerunner for *Cider with Rosie*, Laurie Lee's similarly nostalgic look back at village life in rural Gloucestershire, just across the border from Monmouthshire, which was published nearly two decades later.

Green documents the life of a coal mining village in south Wales through the eyes of our narrator, Huw Morgan, who recalls his life from childhood. Thirty years later, he looks back wistfully to a way of life that is disappearing, as well as out at the world beyond the coal heaps. Huw regularly meditates on time and memory. 'It is very strange to think back like this,' he says at the start of the book, 'although come to think of it, there is no fence or hedge round Time that has gone. You can go back and have what you like if you remember it well enough.'

The episodic plot explores the impact and controversy of the unionisation of the mines (an issue that splits the Morgan family) but also focuses on the tricky relationship issues that Huw's sister Angharad and his sister-in-law Bronwen both face with their respective partners. Another ongoing thread is Huw's love of books – he reads Boswell's *Life of Samuel Johnson* and even has a go at John Stuart Mill's *A System of Logic* as well as visiting a bookshop where he buys copies of *Ivanhoe* and *Treasure Island*. 'O, there is lovely to feel a book, a good book,' he says, 'firm in the hand, for its fatness holds rich promise, and you are hot inside to think of good hours to come.'

The novel is a layered sequence of events, ranging from an amusing lecture on 'the birds and bees' that Huw receives from local preacher Mr Gruffydd, to serious discussions about morality and religion. Sometimes it can feel a little mawkish and err towards a boisterously masculine idea of Christianity.

But the main criticism directed at Llewellyn and the novel seems to be that he rather overexaggerated his own degree of Welshness. He had Welsh parents and certainly identified as Welsh, volunteering to serve in the Welsh Guards in the Second World War. But, despite his claim to have been born in St Davids, Pembrokeshire, he actually came into the world in Hendon and was named Richard Herbert Vivian Lloyd, adopting the middle names 'Dafydd' and 'Llewellyn' later himself. So there were accusations of the author of being a 'professional Welshman' and crafting a certain image for an English audience in painting a clichéd but inaccurate picture of Welsh life.

Similar accusations have also been lobbed at *Cider with Rosie*. Many readers felt that Lee was too young to have remembered some of the events he describes so vividly (though he does point out in his introduction that it is 'a recollection of early boyhood, and some of the facts may be distorted by time'). I'm not sure this really matters in terms of how much enjoyment the reader gets out of *Cider with Rosie*, and I'm even less sure when it comes to a work of fiction like Llewellyn's. It seems harsh to criticise him for using conversations with the local mining community of Gilfach Goch for the book's research and berating him for somehow not being 'properly' Welsh.

As I'm neither Welsh nor a miner, I'm reluctant to offer an expert opinion, but *How Green Was My Valley* is by no means an uncritical sentimental elegy to rural Welsh life ('sentimental' is a criticism which seems to be thrown at this book often, but I'm not sure why sentimentality has to be a bad thing). Mining is graphically shown through the novel to be dangerous, poverty is endemic in Huw's world, violence is accepted as a central part of life (Huw dramatically knocks the stuffing out of an unpleasant teacher), and young unmarried women who become pregnant receive terribly misogynistic treatment. In one of the most brutal episodes, a young girl is 'savaged' on the nearby mountainside. Rather than wait for the law to run its course, Gruffydd organises what is effectively an ethnically motivated witch hunt of the community's 'half-breed

Welsh, Irish, and English' – what Huw describes unpleasantly as 'the living disgust' – to flush out the perpetrator. Once caught, the village's kangaroo court decides it's time for an-eye-for-an-eye retribution, and the culprit is taken up the mountain by the girl's family where he is killed on the spot. The inference is that his body is then burnt as he is unholy. So, the idea that *How Green Was My Valley* offers a romanticised version of rural Wales feels like lazy, shorthand commentary, most likely by people who've not actually read it.

What's made abundantly clear is that the community is proud of being Welsh and regards anyone of English heritage as tainted. English law is sniffed at and the enforcement of the English language rather than the native language provides various flashpoints in the story. While it is written in English, the dialogue mimics Welsh word order so the implication is that all the characters are speaking in Welsh and that we're reading a kind of English translation.

Llewellyn continued Huw's story in three lesser-known sequels in which he emigrates to Patagonia (*Up, into the Singing Mountain*, 1960), experiences the ups and downs of frontier life (*Down Where the Moon is Small*, 1966), and returns back considerably wealthier to Wales and his very changed home valley (*Green, Green My Valley Now*, 1975). I'm not sure I'll attempt these as the ending to *How Green Is My Valley* feels perfect to me, rather like the final page of J. L. Carr's *A Month in the Country*, and I think I'd rather leave Huw's story there.

Why this book matters... it's a regular reference point for discussions about Wales.

Read it because... it's nothing like the film.

Give it a miss if... you prefer novels which aren't so episodic.

What I discovered about Wales... English teachers in Wales weren't all lovely.

BOOK 4

AS ALIEN AS TIBET

◆

I Bought a Mountain
by Thomas Firbank
(1940)

Between wandering around deserted local golf courses and pacing the streets trying to find somewhere selling eggs during the Covid-19 lockdowns, I became gripped by the ongoing BBC television series *Escape to the Country*. Gawping at potential buyers poking their noses into attractive homes in a variety of rural surroundings around the country offered some kind of escapist relief at a time when even walks in the park were rationed. Weighing up the pros and cons of moving from Croydon to deepest Suffolk is one thing, but buying 2,000 acres of hill farm and 3,000 sheep in north Wales when you've no experience of farming is quite another. But that's exactly what the determined twenty-one-year-old Canadian Thomas Firbank did in 1931.

Firbank recorded his experiences of living at his Dyffryn Mymbyr farmhouse (now a National Trust holiday cottage) near Capel Curig over the next half a dozen years in *I Bought a Mountain*. A bestseller at the time of its publication, perhaps because of its escapist appeal to a readership that was by then enduring war, it also marked the beginning of travelogues featuring fretful urbanites heading to the countryside for a better life. 'The rain was a balm, the wind a caress, the wild Welsh mountains were an elemental purge,' he rhapsodises early on. But this is not the 1970s BBC sitcom *The Good Life*, with Tom and Barbara dabbling with small scale self-sufficiency. The chapter 'The Pig Idea' shows we're not in Surbiton. Nor is there much of the humour of the James Herriot sort on show.

Instead, Firbank is bent on throwing himself and his wife into this new world and the task of farming the aforementioned sheep, as well as conquering the surrounding peaks as fast as possible.

What comes across vividly is how hard a farmer's life in hilly Wales was to endure. Firbank is at pains to detail exactly what goes on through a typical year. His book almost works as a manual and, unless you're very interested in agricultural practices, you might find yourself, as I'm afraid I did, whooshing through some sections at speed.

The first three books on my list were very much about Welsh communities from the point of view of the insiders who are part of them. *I Bought a Mountain* is the first written very much from the incomer's perspective. Firbank concedes, 'I was a foreigner in a land as alien to me as Tibet.' He acknowledges that, as an entirely inexperienced outsider, the expert help and advice he receives as the result of cultivating relationships with his neighbours was absolutely essential in making a fist of his project. Whatever issues you might have with him, he is not up for playing at being the hoity-toity lord of the manor.

Firbank is very much the type of chap to tell it like it is. Some comparison could be made to Jeremy Clarkson and his televised efforts to farm in the Cotswolds. Firbank also drifts into the overcooked purple prose territory of his uncle, the novelist Ronald Firbank ('Dyffryn is so strange a mixture of wife and courtesan: loving, wanton, staid, provocative, calm, furious') and is prone to haughty pronouncements ('youth is a glutton, not an epicure'). His tendency to appear rather superior is leavened by an honest appreciation of the people and landscape around him, although my heart rather fell when he offered the opinion that 'The Welshman is not so simple to understand.' However, while it feels like he's describing the mindset of a child, Firbank is actually quite positive about the Welsh, and his appraisal boils down to: be nice and they'll be nice in turn; be a stinker and expect consequences.

Firbank veers between modern progressive views and more conservative takes throughout the book. One moment he is quite reasonably asking why we can't call Snowdon by its Welsh name, Yr Wyddfa, then demanding greater government support for farmers before passionately defending the need for sustainability. The next, he comes up with nonsense like, 'He had a bland red face like a Shropshire man' and comments on the lack of directness among the Welsh by concluding with the sexist view that 'a woman of any nationality has just the same traits' (one wonders what his Welsh mother made of this statement). His tendency to patronise women extends to his wife Esmé (who he describes as having 'the face of an elf ... as dainty as a Dresden shepherdess ... the eager, parted lips of a child and the cool grey eyes of a woman') and what he condescendingly dismisses as her 'ideas' rather than acknowledging their worth. Although he admits that, when their sheep look lost for good in a terrible snowstorm, it's Esmé's determination to dig them out that prevails.

In fact, the book is very much half a story. Esmé is almost as much a background figure as the local shepherds, but there is much more to her. Their marriage ended as war broke out, and Firbank headed off to serve in the army and Japan, only returning to the area in 1993 towards the end of his life. But Esmé stayed working on the farm for the rest of her life and remarried. She also founded the Snowdonia National Park Society and campaigned on a range of issues including safeguarding the red squirrel population on Anglesey. When she died in 1999, she was buried at the farm, close to the sheep pens. As with *In Parenthesis*, reading one book has nudged me down the path of wanting to read another and I've now added her biography to my growing TBR pile.

Why this book matters... it helped start an entire genre of non-fiction.

Read it because... it has less of a colonial feel than you might think.

Give it a miss if... you have a low tolerance for detailed agricultural information.

What I discovered about Wales... there's a large population of red squirrels on Anglesey.

BOOK 5

A RICHARD BURTON FAVOURITE

◆

Raiders' Dawn
by Alun Lewis
(1942)

Well before the advent of social media, successful writers showed themselves cunningly adept at self-promotion, well beyond the pitiful trick of turning one's books with the cover facing out in a bookshop – something I have never done lots of times. The French novelist Stendhal even suggested that 'Great success is not possible without a certain degree of shamelessness.' So, the arrival of photography in the nineteenth century was a boon to early tech adopters such as Charles Dickens, who immediately implemented the concept of the author photo. Nowadays, it's almost de rigueur to have a photo of the author on the cover of books, perhaps to encourage people to see that they are a decent person who'd appreciate some of your hard-earned money if you subscribe to the idea that you should always judge a book by its cover.

Perhaps it's simply an indication of just how shallow I am that I endorse that approach to covers, but the first thing that struck me about my copy of Alun Lewis's *Raiders' Dawn* (a 1945 fifth impression of the first edition with cardboard boards, beige paper wrappers and round end boards) was that the only image on the front cover, taking up two-thirds of it in fact, is a brown and cream engraving of the man himself. Engraver and publisher John Petts, Lewis's friend and colleague, chose a picture of Lewis in three-quarter profile and glancing downwards – like a 1940s Morrissey – as if lost in thought, at the title of the poetry collection. The same image appears on the back cover. And also on the frontispiece. He's everywhere you look. I can't remember ever seeing anything like this on the front of a first edition work of poetry, or indeed fiction. Non-fiction memoir or travelogue, yes. Even Shakespeare had to wait until seven years after his death to get his face on the cover of his *First Folio*. It feels spectacularly egocentric, especially as the thoughtful and public-spirited Lewis was quite the opposite.

At the risk of sounding like a cracked record, Alun Lewis (1915–44) is another writer I'd never come across until making my Welshly list. And again, my ignorance is unjustified as it's not that he's been completely forgotten or that his work is somehow 'difficult'. In his diaries, the actor Richard Burton recounts an occasion when he was trying to tell Elizabeth Taylor how much he loved her and reached for one of his favourite Alun Lewis poems, 'Post-script: For Gweno' (which is included in *Raiders' Dawn*) that starts: 'If I should go away, Beloved'. He rather spoilt the effect by forgetting the rest of the poem after the first line.

> If I should go away,
> Beloved, do not say
> 'He has forgotten me'.
> For you abide,
> A singing rib within my dreaming side;
> You always stay.

Lewis was born and brought up in Cwmaman, a mining village near Aberdare in south Wales. His father was a Welsh-speaker and Lewis regretted not learning the language himself at a time when there was a sharp decline in the number of Welsh-speakers. This comes across in 'The Mountain over Aberdare', an atmospheric depiction of where he grew up. In the very first lines, his feeling of being an insider-outsider is apparent.

> From this high quarried ledge I see
> The place for which the Quakers once
> Collected clothes, my father's home,
> Our stubborn bankrupt village sprawled
> In jaded dusk beneath its nameless hills.

Lewis was part of a loose grouping of Welsh writers in the first half of the twentieth century that wrote in English, which included Lynette Roberts, Brenda Chamberlain, Dylan Thomas and R. S. Thomas, all of whom we will bump into in the following pages. A sensitive man, he had distinctly mixed feelings about the war: he hated fascism but was also a pacifist who disliked many aspects of soldiering. Here is how 'The Sentry' begins:

> I have begun to die.
> For now at last I know
> That there is no escape
> From Night.

The works in the first section of the book are grouped together under the heading 'Poems in Khaki'. In 'All Day It Has Rained', he depicts the mundane realities of daily army life:

> All day it has rained, and we on the edge of the
> moors
> Have sprawled in our bell-tents, moody and dull as
> boors,
> Groundsheets and blankets spread on the muddy
> ground

And from the first grey wakening we have found
No refuge from the skirmishing fine rain
And the wind that made the canvas heave and flap
And the taut wet guy-ropes ravel out and snap.

Just a few lines later he adds a strong contrasting element – still horribly familiar to us eighty years on:

And we talked of girls and dropping bombs on Rome,
And thought of the quiet dead and the loud celebrities
Exhorting us to slaughter, and the herded refugees

Lewis certainly takes on big themes in a very readable and personal way in *Raiders' Dawn*. War looms largest, but here, too, are themes for the ages: love, life and death. My personal favourite lines come in 'Mine Host' where he writes:

Linger not in my library,
If you seek in it wisdom, not pleasure.

At times, they almost feel like song lyrics. As a lifelong fan of the indie pop group The Wedding Present, it strikes me that the book's title poem has something of the same rhythmic lilt as their hit 'My Favourite Dress':

Softly the civilised
Centuries fall
Paper on paper,
Peter on Paul

The poem ends with similar lyricism to the song:

Blue necklace left
On a charred chair

Tells that Beauty
Was startled there.

Lewis died young of a revolver wound to the head, which was officially classed as an accident but widely regarded as the final act in his battle against the depression he suffered from throughout his life.

I enjoyed this book so much that it led me to the first diversion from my programme, to look at his posthumous collection published in 1945 under the splendid title of *Ha! Ha! Among the Trumpets*. Here's the opening of my favourite poem from that book, 'Goodbye', a poignant reflection on the partings caused by war, which was undoubtedly inspired by the last night he spent with his beloved wife Gweno before leaving for war:

So we must say 'Goodbye', my darling,
And go, as lovers go, for ever;
Tonight remains, to pack and fix on labels
And make an end of lying down together.

The poems feel so relevant to our modern situation – surely it's time for the BookTokers to get into Alun Lewis?

Why this book matters... pacifists writing poetry about war are fascinating.

Read it because... if it's good enough for Richard and Liz...

Give it a miss if... pacifists writing poetry about war is not your thing.

What I discovered about Wales... Welsh identity is a complex issue.

BOOK 6

A VILLAGE OF LACE AND STONE

◆

Poems
by Lynette Roberts
(1944)

If you come my way that is…
Between now and then, I will offer you
A fist full of rock cress fresh from the bank
The valley tips of garlic red with dew
Cooler than shallots, a breath you can swank
In the village when you come. At noon-day
I will offer you a choice bowl of cawl
Served with a 'lover's' spoon and a chopped spray
Of leeks or savori fach, not used now,
In the old way you'll understand.

Half a poem in, and I'm hooked.

This is the opening of 'Poem from Llanybri' by Lynette Roberts, the first in her debut collection and a flirtatious invitation to fellow poet Alun Lewis, to whom she had an admitted attraction, to come and see her for a bowl of traditional Welsh soup. Or something.

So far, I've felt pretty bad about never even having heard of five of the first six of the authors on the Welshly list, never mind being able to show off knowledgeably about them in public. I feel a little less ignorant when it comes to Roberts, though. When she died in 1995, she had spent decades suffering from mental health issues, become a Jehovah's Witness, and had long packed up writing and so her work had been all but forgotten already. Her level of obscurity is quite remarkable for a poet who was chums with Edith Sitwell, mentored by Robert Graves, published by T. S. Eliot, had her portrait sketched by Wyndham Lewis, was engaged to Merlin Marshall (one of Ian Fleming's inspirations for James Bond) and whose best man at her wedding was Dylan Thomas.

Roberts (1909–95) is now rightly regarded as one of the finest female war poets. Her prose poem 'Swansea Raid', which is not included in the 2005 *Collected Poems* edition I read, is a particular highlight. 'Poem from Llanybri' is the jauntiest in the collection and the rest of the collection focuses heavily on life in wartime Wales. This is not to say the other poems aren't good; it's just that I'm reminded of all the people whose introduction to the band Green Day was the band's lyrical song 'Good Riddance (Time of Your Life)' and so bought the album *Nimrod* and then felt let down because it was, to put it mildly, not typical of their oeuvre.

Roberts was born and brought up in Buenos Aires. *Poems*, in fact, includes various looks back to her life in Argentina. Her daughter, Angharad Rhys, in the *Collected Poems* preface notes that: 'While she was dying, in rural Wales, she kept reverting to Spanish – though not her first language, it was the language of her childhood. At one point, we needed a dictionary to understand her.' Roberts's family moved to London, where she met Welsh writer and editor Keidrych Rhys. They married at the start of the war and moved to the village of Llanybri in Carmarthenshire, where she threw herself into her new Welsh life. Here is the first stanza from 'Plasnewydd':

You want to know about my village.
You should want to know even if you
Don't want to know about my village.
My village is very small. You could
Pass it with a winning gait.

And from the start, she felt her outsiderishness strongly as she makes clear in the poem 'Lamentation':

To the village of lace and stone
Came strangers. I was one of these

So did the other villagers who come up with the bizarre suspicion that Roberts was a spy while her husband was off at war. In 'Raw Salt on Eye' she writes:

Stone village, who would know that I lived alone:
Who would know that I suffered a two-edged
    pain,
Was accused of spycraft to full innate minds with
    loam,
Was felled innocent, suffered a stain as rare as
    Cain's.

While the human condition is her main concern, there are some superb appreciations in *Poems* of the natural world, especially of birds (in the poems 'Curlew', 'Seagulls', 'Woodpecker' and 'Moorhen') and of the passing of time. In 'The Seasons' she describes how autumn:

Shields the creative mind with covering of leaves,
Settles and matures dormant growth which will
Reappear, under the hard skies of spring.

And like Jones, Roberts is keen to add context to her poems. Her note on 'The Circle of C' is particularly enlightening as I could make no sense of the lines 'But what of my love I cried/As a curlew stabbed the sand'. She explains that this is a reference to a legend about curlews crying at night as they search for the souls of the dead, linking it to the wartime raiders 'droning over estuary and hill, their stiff, ghostly flight barking terror into the hearts of the villagers'. She also explains a connection to dogs in the *Mabinogion*, comparing bombers to the howls of ghost dogs. But Roberts groups them together as notes at the end of the collection rather than regularly sidetracking the reader with fiddly little numbers. The result is that the happy reader can immerse themselves fully in the poetry without distraction and only whizz forward if they feel they need further elucidation. Roberts's notes are also more straightforward than Jones's and actually quite useful. In fact, to be honest, a few more would have been welcome.

The final poem is quite different from the first. 'Cwmcelyn' was originally part of the collection *Gods with Stainless Ears: A Heroic Poem*, published a few years later in 1951. It focuses much more on the experience of war and contains a lot more scattered Welsh language references. It even begins with a long quotation from the Bible's 'Book of Revelation' in Welsh. Roberts's concentration on Welsh heritage is made plain in the notes to this poem, explaining that her intention is to shine a light on the 'culture of another nation'. It's a more complex read than a lot of her work, but again has a fabulous opening:

> Today the same tide leans back, blue rinsing bay,
> With new beaks scissoring the air, a care-away
> Cadence of sight and sound, poets and men
> Rediscovering them. Saline mud
> Siltering, wet with marshpinks, fresh as lime stud

If you listen to the excellent books podcast *Backlisted* (and if you don't, then you have a very pleasant surprise awaiting you), you'll know that the presenters have a thing about not only reading a writer's novels, but moving on to their letters, journals, memoirs, commonplace books, etc. On that same basis, I've added Roberts's *Diaries, Letters and Recollections* to my growing TBR pile, not just because it sounds like it contains a very evocative account of her life in wartime Wales, but because it includes a recollection of visiting T. S. Eliot at his Faber offices in London in 1948. Her small children went bananas during the meeting, tearing up pamphlets and spitting on the floor.

Why this book matters... Roberts is far too good to be a forgotten poet.

Read it because... it offers a firsthand account of being an outsider.

Give it a miss if... you only like poetry that rhymes.

What I discovered about Wales... Swansea was badly bombed during the Second World War.

BOOK 7

TO BEGIN AT THE BEGINNING

◆

Under Milk Wood
by Dylan Thomas
(1954)

This is the one book that nearly everybody mentioned when I asked them to recommend something Welsh, although one of them unenthusiastically described it as 'that weirdy wood thing'. And I wonder how many people have actually read *Under Milk Wood*? My slightly educated guess is that they've actually only *heard* it in the BBC radio play or *seen* it in the stage or film adaptations. I'm a fully paid-up member of 'The Book Is Always Better' club, but even I admit that there are also exceptions. I'd suggest director David Lean's *Doctor Zhivago* beats Boris Pasternak's original novel and that *The English Patient* is far more haunting on the big screen than in Michael Ondaatje's novel. Ditto *The Princess Bride*, *Mary Poppins* and the *Bourne* series. And now that I've listened to *Under Milk Wood* as well as read it, I'd add it to that list of outliers, too.

People enjoy stories in different ways. Like many parents, we discovered that the best way of soothing our three young cherubs/ chimps during long car journeys was to stick on an audio book. The results, for us, were almost instant. It was like we'd mainlined some kind of doping agent into them. We went through every Roald Dahl, *Atticus the Storyteller* by Lucy Coats and read by Simon Russell Beale, and several *How to Train Your Dragon* books (thumbs fully up to David Tennant as narrator). Some we listened to several times, including *Atticus* to the point where the incidental music on the tape becomes a regular earworm for me.

I also loved being read to as a child, though using rather baser technology. I loved reading the Rev. W. Awdry's *Railway Series*, but Johnny Morris's recordings on vinyl were just as memorable, especially as his Thomas the Tank Engine voice sounded like a slightly naughty schoolboy. When I was a bit older, I lapped up the BBC's 1981 radio dramatisation of *The Lord of the Rings* with Stephen Oliver's superb soundtrack. Michael Hordern will always be Gandalf for me, and John le Mesurier is the perfect elderly Bilbo. (For other Tolkien fans I would also strongly recommend hunting down Nicol Williamson's reading of *The Hobbit* in 1974, where he voices all the roles himself. It is available online.)

Nowadays, I rarely listen to audiobooks but that's not because I regard them as some kind of second class substitute for a proper, old-fashioned hardback. After all, the art of storytelling goes back much further than the printed book and, when you listen to *Under Milk Wood*, you can see why. A good reader will bring additional meaning to the text in the way a great actor can bring Shakespeare's characters properly alive on the stage.

I'm glad I went down the audio route with *Under Milk Wood*, which had an early working title of *The Village of the Mad*. I think that being read aloud is how this story of dreams and memory during a day in the life of the residents of a small Welsh fishing village really shines. It is, after all, described by the author as 'a play for voices'. It's one of those stories in which – unlike something like *The Da Vinci Code* – not much happens. But these kinds of stories are often the most revealing and intimate, as anybody who's read R. C. Sherriff's *The Fortnight in September* will acknowledge. Thomas's distinctive, lush, hyphenated language (from the famous 'bible-black' night at the start to the eponymous wood's description as a 'God-built garden' at the end) is a treat to listen to. 'Only your eyes are unclosed to see the black and folded town fast, and slow, asleep,' says the First Voice narrator. Closing my eyes as I listened turned *Under Milk Wood* into a far richer experience.

Although it's certainly a pleasure to read it in the conventional sense, there are plenty of ink-less options available online. I really enjoyed the 1953 recording, the debut reading, in fact, led by Thomas as the stage-setting First Voice narrator. Richard Burton in the 1954 BBC recording makes a rather melodramatic First Voice (I'm afraid I was reminded of Hugh Paddick and Kenneth Connor as the actors giving Prince George lessons on speaking in *Blackadder The Third*) though Hugh Griffith as Captain Cat is excellent. There are film versions, too. Burton returned to the role for the 1972 outing that boasts a very starry cast including, his wife at the time, Elizabeth Taylor, Peter O'Toole, Glynis Johns, Susan Penhaligon and Ruth Madoc. Charlotte Church played Polly Garter in the 2015 version. But for me, the most remarkable is the hypnotic performance in 2021 available from the National Theatre, with Michael Sheen leading the way. His mesmerising opening, which you can easily find online on the National Theatre YouTube channel, really illuminates Thomas's words.

Why this book matters... it's a stone cold classic.

Read it because... the language is an indulgent pleasure whether you listen to it or roll it around in your head via old school print.

Give it a miss if... you think Thomas offers up an unhelpful stereotype of Welsh writing.

What I discovered about Wales... nobody is wholly bad or good.

BOOK 8

CLINT EASTWOOD
OF THE SPIRIT

◆

Song at the Year's Turning
by R. S. Thomas
(1955)

When you make a list in advance for a year-long programme of reading, you really need to think it through, pace yourself and mix it up a bit. I'm not that deft. At this point in the year – and no disrespect to Mr R. S. Thomas (1913–2000) – I felt like I'd maybe read as much poetry as I wanted to read for a little while. I like poetry, but I like other things, too.

However, despite my concerns, *Song at the Year's Turning* proved to be a perfect finale to this run of verse. It is something of an early greatest hits compilation put together by the bestselling poet himself. My 1963 fifth impression (with lovely stone-like cover designed by Judith Bledsoe, one of Robert Graves's earliest muses) contains a very effusive introduction by John Betjeman, who comments on the 'Welshness' of the content.

Betjeman is right. Although there's nothing cosy about this collection – its central questions are about the meaning of life in a changing modern world and the place of God within it – rural Wales is front and centre throughout. Indeed, my copy has been annotated in pencil by a previous owner who methodically went through and translated all the Welsh names in the texts.

Sadly, it's not the copy Ted Hughes bought for his wife, Sylvia Plath, and inscribed 'To Sylvia on her birthday with love from Ted, Oct 27th 1961'. That copy subsequently sold at Bonhams in 2018 for £2,375. Edgar Allan Poe was also a fan of annotating and wrote, 'In getting my books I have always been solicitous of an ample margin; this is not so much through any love of the thing in itself, however agreeable, as for the facility it affords me of pencilling in suggested thoughts, agreements, and differences of opinion, or brief critical comments in general.' I feel the same, but I like *light* annotations. I have a copy of J. R. R. Tolkien's translation of *Sir Gawain and the Green Knight* that is virtually unreadable as somebody has inserted an almost word-for-word translation in the line gaps between the text. But a few notes here and there add to the copy's journey through readers. In my copy of R. S. Thomas, the unknown annotator limits himself to ticking half a dozen poems in the contents pages, presumably favourites, with no additional comment. It's simply a little note for me, the unknown future reader, about what he took from the book. I like feeling part of that chain.

Though Thomas was a keen naturalist, his work is the opposite of traditional pleasant pastoral poetry. It's serious stuff and not the kind of material that offers up many soundbites for Visit Wales to welcome in tourists. He was also a contradictory character, furiously criticising the English for, what he saw as, the destruction of the Welsh nation, and yet sending his son to an English public school. Though he could be very supportive, many regarded him as a sourpuss (Philip Larkin, admittedly also not notorious for his bonhomie, referred to him in letters as 'Arsewipe Thomas'). Seamus Heaney, fellow nominee and winner of the Nobel Prize in Literature in 1995 (R. S. Thomas was nominated by the Welsh Academy in 1996), summed him up as 'a kind of Clint Eastwood of the spirit'. Indeed, Thomas initially refused the nomination and only caved in on the basis that, if he won, he would be able to give his acceptance speech in Welsh.

Thomas's sombreness was reflected in his very direct and deceptively simple style. No footnotes are needed with his poetry and you don't need to have a good working knowledge of the *Mabinogion* to understand what he is saying. Often, his work is very filmic, too. A good example is 'Cynddylan on a Tractor' which starts:

> Ah, you should see Cynddylan on a tractor.
> Gone the old look that yoked him to the soil;

But while Cynddylan, a farmer, is delighted with his new vehicle, Thomas is more concerned that his investment in the white heat of technology is scaring off the local wildlife.

> Riding to work now as a great man should,
> He is the knight at arms breaking the fields'
> Mirror of silence, emptying the wood
> Of foxes and squirrels and bright jays.
> ...
> And all the birds are singing, bills wide in vain,
> As Cynddylan passes proudly up the lane.

Thomas was, to put it mildly, distrustful of, what he regarded as, inessential gadgets. He was also an Anglican priest and dedicated himself to his work in various rural parishes of, what was then, Montgomeryshire in mid-Wales, where he took the opportunity to give sermons demonising washing machines, televisions and fridges.

What he doesn't do in these poems is disrespect the farmers and parishioners he writes about, nor denigrate the bleak landscape in which they survive. We first meet his Welsh everyman, Iago Prytherch, in the poem 'The Peasant' on page twenty-one of my copy of the collection:

> Just an ordinary man of the bald Welsh hills,
> Who pens a few sheep in a gap of cloud

Iago spends his evenings at home spitting into the fire. Thomas admires his indomitable spirit in the face of adverse weather:

> Remember him, then, for he, too, is a winner of
> wars,
> Enduring like a tree under the curious stars.

Iago reappears in 'Memories' on page forty-five.

> Come, Iago, my friend and let us stand together
> Now in the time of the mild weather

Thomas goes on to celebrate the countryman's experience-led knowledge of farming and nature ('Your secret learning, innocent of books') and his 'heart's rich harvest'. It's a movingly authentic declaration of admiration. We see Iago for the final time in the collection on page ninety-nine in 'Lament for Prytherch'. He is now an older and richer farmer, his 'barns oozing corn like honey'. But his hard life out in the fields is catching up with him physically.

> Your heart that is dry as a dead leaf
> Undone by frost's cruel chemistry
> Clings in vain to the bare bough
> Where once in April a bird sang.

Thomas wrote plenty more poetry after *Song at the Year's Turning*. Of the little I've read beyond this collection, I particularly liked 'A Marriage' from his 1992 poetry collection *Mass for Hard Times*. The poem was dedicated to his wife, Elsi, who died the year before. It starts by describing how they met fifty years previously and how they'd moved through their time together, from their first kiss to the appearance of wrinkles on her face. It made me feel quite weepy.

Why this book matters... it's an ideal opportunity to experience the mind of one of the best winners of the Nobel Prize we *never* had.

Read it because... you'll struggle to find a more accessible book of quality poetry.

Give it a miss if... you want a cheerfully cosy read.

What I discovered about Wales... it can enchant all kinds of people.

BOOK 9

NOT LOST IN TRANSLATION

◆

The Awakening
by Kate Roberts
(2006)

◆

Translated from the Welsh *Y Byw Sy'n Cysgu* (1956)
and previously translated into English
under the title *The Living Sleep*

It's been pretty rural reading so far. There have been a lot of sheep and plenty of valleys. So it's with some relief that I venture into a town setting and headlong into a whole new set of issues that don't involve tractors. In fact, the start of this book is probably the nearest the Welshly list has come to an episode of *EastEnders* so far.

Lora Ffenig's seemingly happy eleven-year marriage smacks into the rocks – and early doors, too. On page three, she discovers her husband, Iolo, has run off Dirty Den-style with his boss's housekeeper (cue the 'doof, doof, drum roll'), leaving her with their two children, some in-laws she's not fond of at all and a polite male admirer.

So far, so Albert Square, but that's where any similarity ends.

Rather than burning down garages or pushing people off cliffs, the novel follows Lora's stoic efforts to gradually come to terms with this sudden change in her circumstances and adapt to her new life.

Indeed, there's also nothing soap-opera-like about Roberts's precise, understated style. In fact, the book rather reminded me of Penelope Fitzgerald, especially *The Bookshop*. I'm tempted to describe *The Awakening* as unemotional, but Roberts's style could have another explanation. One of the other interesting things about this book is that it's the first on my list which was originally written in Welsh, so the book I read is a translation.

Jorge Luis Borges, who had a remarkable command of English as well as Spanish, argued that it was wrong to suggest that translation is necessarily inferior to the original. 'The concept of the "definitive text" corresponds only to religion or exhaustion,' he said (he also claimed to be puzzled by his huge reputation in English-speaking nations and joked that he was clearly being improved upon in English translation). It's my loss that I cannot read it in the original Welsh. Having said that, this English translation by novelist Siân James feels very natural. The novel reads convincingly as an English text, a delicate balancing act between remaining faithful to the meaning, style and voice of the original and recreating a fresh new text in another language.

Some years ago, I interviewed Spanish novelist Ángela Vallvey about her comic novel *A la caza del último hombre salvaje*, which became *Hunting the Last Wild Man* in English translation. While she acknowledged that the book was still *hers*, she regarded the English rendering as the translator's version. 'Whether it's changed or not is not the most important thing. What is important is that it can be read in another language with pleasure and without struggle. Perhaps it might lose some of its uniqueness and quintessence, but it's enriched by the words of the other language, never impoverished by them.' Cervantes called translation 'the other side of the tapestry', which feels, to me, close to the mark.

However Lora comes across in Welsh, in English, she's respectable and dignified, if perhaps a little distant. It's clear that Iolo has left her for somebody he finds significantly jollier. Initially, she's even rather understanding of her husband's choice.

> This much could be said for Iolo Ffennig, he had dared to break away from the monotony of life to have a love affair. They were all country people, and Welsh at that, and Welsh people couldn't usually enjoy pleasure because they were religious, and couldn't enjoy religion because they longed to pursue their appetites.

That understanding hits rather a brick wall when it turns out he's done something actually criminal.

Roberts charts – partly through the private thoughts of the diary she regularly keeps up – how Lora 'wakes up'. 'I've been able to express something that I've been prevented from saying by the society I live in,' Lora writes in one entry. And it's a society clearly incapable of dealing with the situation. 'No one had much to say,' Lora observes soon after her abandonment has been made public. 'This was different from a death. One had the right words for the wife of a dead man, but none for the wife of a man who'd deserted her.'

Then there's the social stigma. Iolo's boss, Aleth Meurig, is patently keen on Lora and she realises that she 'must be on her guard, and remember that she was still a married woman and it was Wales she lived in. But there, whatever she did, people were sure to talk.' And talk they do when Meurig visits her at her home, however innocent the meeting. The local priest turns up specifically to advise Lora against it happening again.

Lora's awakening is not a sudden sea change, it's a matter of small steps. At one social gathering, she is offered a cigarette and hesitates. She only accepts after her son encourages her ('Take it, Mam, and enjoy yourself.'). A friend tells her that she should 'Begin that habit of showing people you don't care what they think.'

By Lora's final diary entry, the change is, if not exactly complete, certainly noticeable. 'I feel I've really got to know myself better,' she says. 'I see that I have, by hardening myself, grown, and that I have within myself a spring which will continue to rise and give me an incentive to live.'

I've been writing as though Kate Roberts (1891–1985) is some kind of minor, lucky dip find that I unearthed through extensive research and am now holding up triumphantly to the literary light. The truth is that she's generally acclaimed to be the leading Welsh female novelist and short story writer of the last century with an impressive back catalogue of titles full of major female characters. It's surely time for a revival.

Why this book matters... it explores an emotional challenge without resorting to overblown hysteria.

Read it because... Lora is a finely created character.

Give it a miss if... gently restrained novels are absent from your bookshelves.

What I discovered about Wales... small towns are the same everywhere.

BOOK 10

IN SHORT

◆

A Toy Epic
by Emyr Humphreys
(1958)

I am a sucker for a lengthy epic read, whether it's the hefty single volume of Vikram Seth's *A Suitable Boy*, the five that make up Elizabeth Jane Howard's *Cazalet Chronicles*, or the apparently never-ending volumes imagining Tolkien's Middle-earth. What I've not read is a short epic.

Nearly twenty years in the making, Humphreys's coming-of-age novel first appeared in Welsh as *Y Tri Llais* (The Three Voices) and as a radio play before it became *A Toy Epic* in English. According to M. Wynn Thomas in the introduction to my 1989 Seren edition, the 'epic' was a hangover from when the author had first planned it out as a novel in verse and the 'toy' was a reference to the age of its schoolboy protagonists. But it must also partly be a nod to its length because it's more novella than epic: of the 200 pages, thirty-five are the introduction and the afterword, both written by M. Wynn Thomas (I'm not much one for too much explanation of a story, but these are both genuinely illuminating and interesting), seven more are bibliography and notes, and forty are in an appendix which is a fragment of an earlier version of the text (the whole work was intended to be longer and has never been published), leaving just 104 pages of story.

This story focuses on three young boys in Flintshire, northeast Wales, near the English border. The aftershocks of the First World War are still apparent at the start and the approach of the Second World War is hurtling towards them by the end. Michael, Albie and Iorwerth, each represent different strands of interwar Welsh life. Michael is a privileged Welsh-deriding churchman's son. Iorwerth is from a chapel-going Welsh nationalist family. And Albie is the son of a working-class bus conductor who feels speaking Welsh will just saddle his offspring with a badge of inferiority. We watch them grow and change – there's a nice minor allusion to this when they study Ovid's *Metamorphoses* at school together – as they head towards the prospect of university. They deal with everything from homosexuality and class war to religious beliefs and the diverse possibilities of Welsh identity.

What is interesting about *A Toy Epic* is that we don't watch the characters; we *hear* them. The novel is a three-way stream of consciousness, although more along the lines of Virginia Woolf's *Mrs Dalloway* or *The Waves* than Molly Bloom's finale in James Joyce's *Ulysses*. It's a very emotional, very honest book about young boys – and Wales itself – trying to plot their place in a world where fate seems to have a dampening effect on free will.

Humphreys certainly packs a lot in his hundred pages and I suspect readers will either love or hate it rather than come away thinking it was simply ok. In short, I loved it.

Why this book matters... it offers various perspectives on how Wales was developing in the middle of the twentieth century.

Read it because... it's a thoughtful take on the coming-of-age story.

Give it a miss if... you're in the mood for a multi-volume saga.

What I discovered about Wales... the use of the Welsh language within Wales has been an issue for longer than I thought.

BOOK 11

COMING HOME

◆

Border Country
by Raymond Williams
(1960)

The overused dictum 'Never judge a book by its cover' is, as Hamlet was fond of pointing out, more honoured in the breach than in the observance. In the same way that most of us place more confidence in a cleverly designed wine label than one which looks like somebody's nephew has thrown it together in Microsoft Paint, a book's cover really matters. It is why publishers constantly republish and rebrand titles with new and enticing covers. And it is why Jeanette Winterson, who objected to the blurbs on her newly rejacketed novels, publicly burnt a selection of them and posted it to social media. It is why Penguin has sold millions of its *Clothbound Classics* series in countries around the world.

On first glance, the cover of my 1988 Hogarth Press paperback of *Border Country* looks nothing special. It's a hand-drawn illustration by Amy Burch of a boy and a middle-aged railway worker standing in front of a railway signal box against a backdrop of blue sky and undulating green fields. Nice enough, a bit old-fashioned looking now, perhaps, compared to the sometimes quite garish covers of many modern titles. Looking at other editions, they also go with a combination of trains and signal boxes on the cover, which is hardly surprising since the railways are central to the story. But the 1988 one is very special because the signalman's face is a portrait of the author, the academic and cultural critic Raymond Williams, as he looked in the late 1980s and not when he wrote it decades earlier.

It's an unusual approach (I can't think of any other novel's cover which portrays the writer as one of the characters – please do tell me if you can) but very appropriate in this instance since the book is based on Williams's own experience of growing up in Wales. While we've met several characters who were newcomers and outsiders to Wales during our literary journey, this is the first book that concentrates on a protagonist leaving Wales and then what it feels like to return west of the border.

The story focuses on two generations of the Prices, a working-class family living in south Wales, close to the border with England, whose lives are linked to the railway line that passes through their village. In the present day, Matthew is a relatively young academic in London who returns home to Glynmawr (a fictional village inspired by the author's hometown of Pandy. If you look online, you'll find a photograph of Raymond Williams standing in front of the signal box at Pandy that shows you how good the cover portrait is) after his father, Harry, has a stroke. Matthew's parents' story – which includes his own coming-of-age segment – is told in extended flashbacks with a particular emphasis on the 1926 General Strike and its fallout. A key character is family friend Morgan Prosser, a devoted union man who becomes disillusioned with the workers' struggle and pessimistically forecasts 'a slow and shocking cancellation of the future'.

There are lots of borders in the novel, both geographic and psychological, as well as cultural and economic, with lots of lines to be crossed, recrossed and blurred (I hesitate to use the term 'liminal' as everything seems to be described as liminal nowadays). Old and young have to go on a journey, as do miners and train workers. Even the young Harry is at odds with his older landlord who can't see the point of railways: 'Where do they want to be going, all them up and down in these trains? They only go, after, to come back.'

There's a particularly poignant Welsh word that's used a lot: *hiraeth*. It doesn't translate exactly into English but is something along the lines of a bittersweet nostalgic homesickness for home – specifically Wales itself. At the start of the book, when we meet Matthew, he is suffering from a kind of academic's block in his research into migration in nineteenth-century Welsh coalfields and he absolutely does not feel this kind of pull to his homeland. But as the tale progresses, he begins to come to terms with the two quite different pieces of his life, a dichotomy emphasised by being known as Matthew in England, his officially registered name, but as Will in Wales, since his mother wanted to name him William instead.

In the most basic way, it's a novel about exploring a sense of place, which is really at the heart of what my reading programme is all about and probably why I enjoyed it so much. Williams has explicitly said as much: 'I was trying to make a contrast between two ways of seeing the same place.' In London, Matthew describes himself as 'The man on the bus, the man in the street, but I am Price from Glynmawr, and here, understandably, that means very little.' But when he returns to his home, he realises that he has, this time, 'come as a stranger: accept that'. In leaving for London, Matthew not only crosses one border and into a kind of self-exile, but he then returns, and then... well, I promised no spoilers. What I will say is that, for me, this is the first book on the list that feels like it's grappling with what it really means to be Welsh in the modern age. I liked *A Toy Epic*, but it feels a bit didactic when measured against *Border Country*, which feels much more of a practical and human exploration.

Although Williams does sometimes drum home the 'borders' theme a bit strongly – an argument about the working class is noted by the narrator as 'a border defined, a border crossed', ok, ok, we get it – the novel is also a rather moving account of how a family communicates or fails to communicate. Matthew berates his parents for their disinclination to discuss important subjects, which makes it all the more endearing when his father says to him on his return home, 'I can't say all I want, Will. But I want you to know it's made a world of difference, you coming.'

Why this book matters... it's a fine introduction to the crucial concept of *hiraeth*.

Read it because... Williams was an important commentator on all matters Welsh.

Give it a miss if... you don't want to muse about where you grew up as opposed to where you live now (though, even then, you *should* read it).

What I discovered about Wales... the central part that the railways played in Wales's modern story.

BOOK 12

UP ON THE ORME LAST NIGHT

◆

Jampot Smith
by Jeremy Brooks
(1960)

In the introduction, we explored a few methods for choosing your next read and here's another one – look for books that feature places you know and like. While I don't have a dedicated shelf of these, a quick whizz along my bookcase reveals plenty of titles that I've chosen based, at least partly, on their geo-literary location. So my early childhood in Shropshire is represented by Jonathan Coe's *The Rain Before it Falls* (Much Wenlock), Melissa Harrison's *At Hawthorn Time* evokes the little market town I lived in until I was thirteen, Wellington, in the novel's setting Ardleton. In *Rain*, Harrison walks around the Wrekin, the big hill just outside Wellington. York, where I spent the remainder of my teenage years, features on my bookshelves via Kate Atkinson's *Behind the Scenes at the Museum* and *Sovereign* by C. J. Sansom (the one where Shardlake meets Henry VIII). I've also lived in Oxford (*Gaudy Night* by Dorothy L. Sayers), Madrid (*Leaving the Atocha Station* by Ben Lerner) and St Albans (*Crooked Heart* by Lissa Evans).

Jampot Smith is set in Llandudno on the north Wales coast. Although I've never lived there, it was where we spent several holidays when I was young, including one particularly memorable year when I cut my toes quite badly on a shard of buried glass on the

58

beach. But I bear no grudge and have to admit that I pencilled in this book largely because a friend mentioned it features the Great Orme headland, which has a marvellous tramway to the top. As a seven-year-old, I remember thinking it was the best thing ever. And geography is as clearly as good a way as any to pick a book because this coming-of-age story (you don't read one for years and then three come along all at once) is quietly excellent.

Bernard, also known as 'Jampot Smith' – a reference to his slightly undeserved reputation as a young Don Juan – is a kind of nice, middle-class everyboy on the verge of everymanhood. Over the course of about two years, he hangs out with his friends, plays a lot of records and, in true sensitive teenager fashion, tries to come to terms with some really Big Ideas about love, war, and good versus evil.

Yes, this is another war book as the book takes place during the Second World War. Initially, his group of friends are merely playing at being soldiers, but the feel of war is pervasive. His friend Epsom describes the bombing of Liverpool, which they can just about make out across the bay: "'I was up on the Orme last night," said Epsom. "You could see the fires burning. Sometimes it was just a dull red glow, and then there'd be a sudden sort of explosion of fire, and sometimes a lot of explosions all together.'" By the end of the book, the group are making adult choices about heading to war or choosing pacifism.

Bernard mirrors the author's own experience of being evacuated from the south of England to Llandudno with his family during the early days of the Second World War. Indeed, Brooks based several characters on people he knew, placing this book in the fictional memoir category.

After the success of *Jampot Smith*, his second novel, he spent several years as the literary manager of the Royal Shakespeare Company under Peter Hall. Wales clearly remained close to his heart as his output included a semi-musical version of Dylan Thomas's *A Child's Christmas in Wales*, a book which is not in the Welshly reading project but which I reread and listen to every yuletide. He also returned later with his wife Eleanor, a painter, to live not far from the town in a village called Gelli, in the Rhondda Fawr valley.

Brooks uses his local knowledge, lightly but tellingly, by including street names quite naturally in the text ('After that, I began to see this girl about everywhere: in the school, on the beach, outside the library, or simply cycling quietly along, alone, down the Conway Road on some unguessable errand.'). This really brings the setting alive, and, even though it's an Englishman writing about an English boy, it anchors the story firmly to a concrete Wales setting rather than a place that has more of an abstract Welsh feel to it.

Jampot Smith also has a scene that is a fine antidote to the *Literary Review* magazine's annual Bad Sex Award. There is plenty of hormonal teenage angst in the book, but after seemingly endless and charmingly adolescent 'will they, won't they' Ross and Rachel-type shenanigans (but gratifyingly not over an entire decade and ten seasons), Bernard and his girlfriend, Kathy, find themselves alone. Their teenage fumblings make for several pages of wonderfully authentic and cringemaking reading for those who remember the torture of being a teenager in love.

Why this book matters… the writing about teenage relationships is wonderfully accurate.

Read it because… there's a marvellous section about playing records on a gramophone.

Give it a miss if… you find hormonal youngsters a bit cringe.

What I discovered about Wales… Llandudno is much nearer Liverpool than I realised.

BOOK 13

A CLANDESTINELY BORROWED SAUSAGE VAN

◆

Place of Stones
by Ruth Janette Ruck
(1961)

The cover of my first edition, second impression copy of *Place of Stones* published by Faber & Faber is, and I don't say this lightly, the dullest of any book I have ever read. The bottom third is taken up by the title, printed in white on brown, plus a thick white strip with the author's name in black. The top third is a black-and-white photograph of Ruth Janette Ruck dressed in open-toed sandals, a sensible, calf-length, A-line skirt, and a white blouse. She is hoeing what looks like a field full of stones, her head down, concentrating on the work so that we cannot see her face. I would have liked to have been in the marketing meeting when it was decided that this image would be the one to shift lorryloads of books about sheep farming in Wales. Later editions go wild and swap the cover photo for one of a group sheep shearing session, an image included in my edition on page eighty-one. Another new edition features the same image but rendered by an artist as a drawing on the cover. Times have changed in the publishing biz.

It's not only the front cover that's a bit special. The foreword is written by George Henderson, who is regularly namechecked in the text as a sage source of advice, and a famous Cotswolds farming guru of the time. He gives *Place of Stones* a glowing write-up. 'This book delights me,' he enthuses. 'Not only is it well written, which means that interest is steadily built up throughout, but it drives home many of my cherished principles of farming without appearing to do so.' Interested in finding out more about those principles? Look no further than the inside back-cover flap, which, instead of carrying Ruck's biographical details and photograph, gives plenty of space to three of George's own books, all also published by Faber: *The Farming Ladder*, *Farmer's Progress* ('surely the best book on farming ever written' says *Poultry Breeder*) and *The Farming Manual*. Nothing like keeping it in the family.

I put this book on the Welshly list, not for the remarkable ordinariness of its frontage but because it covers very similar ground to the first 'back to the land' book I read in the already dim and distant past: book four of our journey – *I Bought a Mountain*. In fact, it's literally similar ground since Ruck's farm was just around the corner from where Firbank had his farm. How far have we come in the two intervening decades?

Ruck comes to farming at a young age and builds a genuine interest. Like Firbank, her family buy the farm in 1946 although their motivation seems to be a bit of a whim when they admire it while on holiday – rather than an attempt to escape the rat race. Like Firbank, it was a huge change of lifestyle. 'We bought the farm, and burned the boats of the life we had always known,' she writes, very matter-of-factly. On the farm, Ruck develops an interest in climbing and, while there's a lot of detail about the day-to-day work of a farmer in the 1950s, it's not a handbook on farming. It feels sincere, with as many failures chronicled as successes, and the pages hum with her energetic determination.

There are two main differences between Ruck and Firbank's experiences. First, Firbank acknowledged but still rather slid over the contribution to his success made by his wife, Esmé. Collaboration is the entire enterprise from Ruck's point of view. She hired help and later her husband, Paul, is very present if enigmatically quiet. She also has plenty of help from neighbouring farmers – which she readily declares – but it's her show, no doubt. Like Firbank, she's frank about the highs and lows of her rural lifestyle, but while she explains what she's doing and why to the reader, it's done in a modest way. There's a lot less of the theatrical mansplainer about her tone, although, as a result, it's also less dramatic and much milder. Even when Ingrid Bergman rather unexpectedly turns up to shoot a movie, *The Inn of Sixth Happiness*, Ruck seems more excited about the fact that Twentieth Century Fox is paying her a fiver a day to drive cast and crew around the area in her rickety jeep than the presence of a Hollywood star.

Secondly, there are pictures accompanying Ruck's text. A really attractive hand-drawn map of the area by Paul, and black-and-white photos of the buildings and of the author at work dotted throughout. One of them appears to have been taken at the same time as the photo on the cover, only it seems that she is not hoeing a field of stones but one of strawberries. I know it's a small thing, but I enjoyed seeing pictures of the area she was writing about, and they helped me stop wincing every time she eagerly described how she was using asbestos sheeting for her building work.

If you like this book, then Ruck followed *Place of Stones* with two more volumes accounting her experiences in western Snowdonia: *Hill Farm Story* and *Along Came a Llama*. I've only flicked through these, but they are much the same and have some likeable details in them – like her decison to turn the henhouse into a writing hut and her admission that she read during meals, rather than chatting to her husband since they would spend the whole day with each other. And if you want still more, her sixteenth-century farm cottage Tŷ-Mawr is now available as a holiday let.

If that isn't enough to entice you to enter into the world of Jane Ruck then I offer you this quote: 'About five o'clock, Mr. B arrived with a friend, in what I sensed was a clandestinely-borrowed sausage van.' Anything which contains this sentence demands to be read.

Why this book matters... it's a matter-of-fact, realistic account rather than an energetically enthusiastic incomer's memoir.

Read it because... the Ingrid Bergman section is superbly understated and unstarry-eyed.

Give it a miss if... you're in the mood for a rip-roaring action adventure.

What I discovered about Wales... it's been on Hollywood location scouts' minds for a long time.

BOOK 14

PERHAPS THE GREATEST WELSH NOVEL

◆

One Moonlit Night
(Un Nos Ola Leuad)
by Caradog Prichard
(1961)

In 2014, the *Wales Arts Review*'s contest to settle, once and for all, what is the 'greatest Welsh novel' ended with a win on points rather than a clear knockout. The winner was the short-ish *One Moonlit Night (Un Nos Ola Leaud)* by Caradog Prichard. So it would have been contrary of me to leave it off the Welshly reading list. It would also have been a big mistake. Because it's outstanding.

It's also very odd.

'I'll go and ask Huw's Mam if he can come out to play,' is the inviting and fairly straightforward opening line. After that, we're catapulted immediately into the life of an unnamed little boy who is the narrator of the ups and downs (mostly downs and often right-downs) of life in the slate quarrying village of Bethesda in the early twentieth century. This is not the sunlit uplands; it's a story which makes Barry Hines's *A Kestrel for a Knave* look like *Cider with Rosie*. Think Patrick McCabe's *The Butcher Boy* in Wales.

In the next dozen or so pages, we're confronted with child abuse; a suicide in a toilet; domestic violence; a flasher; a man suffering an epileptic fit in the street; and a couple having sex in the woods. It doesn't let up after that either, really. As we hop around meeting the village's other residents in an episodic *Under Milk Wood*-style, the main story arc is the worsening of the boy's mother's mental illness.

Adding to the turmoil is that, after a while, it's obvious that the boy is actually only narrating part of the story once he has grown up. There is a second narrator – a kind of presence called alternately the Queen of the Black Lake or the Queen of Snowdon or the self-styled Bride of the Beautiful One, who may or may not be connected to the village's history of Christian revival. As Jan Morris says in her brief afterword, 'it all feels rather like a dream'. Indeed, Prichard himself described the book as 'an unreal picture, seen in the twilight and in the light of the moon'.

I had no idea how the story was going to end and found myself thinking if it was going to end something like Flann O'Brien's *The Third Policeman*. It doesn't, but it is a very odd ending indeed, which leaves you wondering what on earth you've just read. There's an excellent translator's note by Philip Mitchell in my 2015 Canongate edition that explains how he went about his work. It must have been quite an experience to spend so much time living with this book.

In fact, it's not a dream, more of an experimental autobiographical exorcism. Like *Border Country* it is a personal portrait of childhood but just much, *much* darker. Prichard lived in extreme poverty in Bethesda as a child and saw his mother committed to Denbigh Mental Hospital for her ongoing issues. There's one particularly heartbreaking scene near the end of the book when the boy has to deal with his mother's deteriorating condition and it feels like it was drawn from terrible personal experience.

Prichard became a journalist and then a very successful poet, but *One Moonlit Night* was, like *To Kill a Mockingbird*, *Wuthering Heights* and *Gone with the Wind*, a one-hit wonder. It's almost like it provided him with a means of coming to terms with his childhood and that, once complete, he had no need to write further fiction.

I realise that all this is unlikely to encourage you to pick this book up. But while almost every page could carry a trigger warning, it's not bleak misery-lit. The boy narrator guides us in a remarkably robust, perky, almost detached manner around his world and recounts what's going on around him as just normal everyday events. There are some very funny scenes including one at a local football match. There are also touching scenes and the boy's relationship with his friends is beautifully observed. Throughout, the writing is mesmerising. If Max Porter had written his engaging 2019 folk prose-poem-novel *Lanny* sixty years ago, I suspect it might have looked a little like this.

One Moonlit Night is a great book, certainly, but I'm not sure it's the greatest Welsh novel. And, while I enjoyed it immensely, I can certainly say that, fourteen books into the Welshly list, I'm starting to yearn for something that isn't about a little Welsh village.

Why this book matters... it's hard to imagine anything in the rest of the list feeling quite so Welsh.

Read it because... In fact **reread** it, as the book needs thinking about so carefully that one reading is probably not enough (well, not for me anyway).

Give it a miss if... you're a stickler for correct punctuation.

What I discovered about Wales... I'd forgotten the importance of the slate industry to Wales (the book actually stirred me to track down a little boxed set of a dozen examples of rocks that I bought on holiday there when I was at primary school, and it made me slightly weepy with nostalgia).

BOOK 15

HOW WE MOURN

◆

The Small Mine
by Menna Gallie
(1962)

Almost inevitably, this one's set in a village, too. Commentator's curse.

It takes some skill to kill off your leading man in a novel and still keep the reader on board, but Gallie manages this with some panache in *The Small Mine*. If that feels like a rotten spoiler, I apologise but, in my defence, the blurb on the back of my Honno Classics 2000 edition gives the game away in the first sentence. 'First published in 1962, this novel tells the tale of a young collier's death in a mining accident in Cilhendre, a fictional industrial village in the south Wales valleys.' Don't blame the messenger.

The handsome and popular but extremely doomed Joe Jenkins doesn't make it past page eighty-four (I won't say *how* he dies to keep up some minor element of suspense). But although Joe is the character around which the novel revolves – I'm envisioning Iwan Rheon playing him in the film version – the book's not really about him.

There's plenty to enjoy here: varying views on the fairly recent nationalisation of the coal industry, some political to-ing and fro-ing, an excellent portrayal of a thoughtful and experienced miner who's been invalided out of work (perhaps played by Michael Sheen?), and a marvellous set-piece bonfire celebration on Guy Fawkes Night near the end. And, far from fizzling out, it also has a cracking ending, which rather reminded me of noir film *The Third Man*. Without giving the game away, *The Small Mine* is also the kind of mystery story where the characters are left largely in the dark about whodunnit while the reader sees all and knows all.

Of course mining plays a central role, too, especially the kind of small mine that nationalisation effectively shut down. Gallie (also the translator of Caradog Prichard's *One Moonlit Night*) writes very atmospherically about her work – she apparently did a couple of eight-hour shifts underground to get a feel for life in a mine and the effects of it on the miners and the wider community:

> They went on; the crouching mile, two, three miles to the cage and the electric lights; the bottom, a whitewashed cavern, archlighted, vast, inhuman. Here they waited, tired, patient, black, eight hours of coal and darkness heavy on their shoulders and on the thin backs of their necks. The air was thick and artificial, like food out of cans. The cage came down, was filled, came down, filled, took up its load; the walls went spinning by, close, slimy, shining, fast. And on the top it was autumn.

This is also the first book on our list that looks at twentieth-century war in the rear-view mirror. It is the 1950s and the English are regular incomers, but we also have young German miners. Joe has to fight to hold back his xenophobic feelings about the old enemy but his friend and sometime lover, Sall, is much more sympathetic: 'That's ancient history now, Joe, and anyway, most of those chaps are too young to know anything about it.' This is typical of Gallie's even-handed narrative approach throughout the novel, which extends even to one of the least likeable characters who comes to play a major part in the story.

Aberystwyth-based Honno Press was set up in 1986 to publish literature by and about Welsh women to a bigger audience, and this was its third title in a still ongoing series. It's easy to see why Honno chose to republish *The Small Mine* because what makes the story particularly engaging is Gallie's focus on the women in the mining community. The book shows a community on the cusp, with traditional older values and approaches to life giving way to a new generation's attitudes and this is represented through the female characters.

We have Joe's mother, Flossie, (possibly played by Pam Ferris?), who runs a tight ship domestically and delightedly fusses over her only child. The archetypal traditional mother, she lives for him so entirely – as she is expected to do – that she is completely devastated at his death and is reduced to muttering 'He was the apple of my eye' as an automatic reply to those offering condolences. Then we have the younger, previously married and politely promiscuous Sall (maybe I would cast Joanna Page or Eve Myles, who was actually born in the same village as Gallie, Ystradgynlais). Although she is, in some ways, less traditional than Flossie, she's still constrained by society's unwritten rules. As his occasional lover, she feels unable to mourn Joe's death openly and even buys roses for his funeral, only to throw them away because she is worried about what people will think. And then we have Cynthia, Joe's kind-of girlfriend (perhaps played by Alexa Davies?). She has her own job, knows her own mind and, when the worst happens, refuses to be pigeonholed as the bereaved almost-bride. Instead, she determines her own future and it's her who has the last word and last action of the book.

Perhaps it's simply that this and the previous book are set

closer to the date when I was born, and I can identify with the characters more strongly than those from earlier books, but this feels increasingly like the advent of a new society. This change is implied at the bonfire when an old bardic chair is ceremonially burned. Joe's liking for swanky Italian shoes, money and holidays also offers a strong contrast to his parents' fairly limited ambitions. Yes, there are women in *How Green Was My Valley* and *The Battle to the Weak* who are spirited and determined, but they're still very much powerless within their society, whereas, in Cynthia, we see a young woman in control of her own life even in the face of tragedy.

I liked this so much that I immediately added another Gallie (1919–90) to the list, not the Cilhendre prequel (*Strike for a Kingdom*) that came out before *The Small Mine*, but *Travels with a Duchess*, which looks like lots of fun. And isn't set in a village.

Why this book matters... it puts women at the centre of a story about coal mining.

Read it because... it's got an ending on a par with the film The Third Man.

Give it a miss if... you like the suspense of a whodunnit.

What I discovered about Wales... the existence of small private mines about which I knew nothing and the tension between them and the nationalised ones.

BOOK 16
CREATORS AND CREATIONS
◆
The Twelve Dancers
by William Mayne
(1962)

I suspect that there will be various reasons for *not* reading one of the books on my Welshly list, and by the end of paragraph three, I suspect many of you may have decided this is one you're going to pass on.

The year 1962 was an unusually good one for children's books with the publication of Joan Aiken's *The Wolves of Willoughby Chase*, *A Wrinkle in Time* by Madeleine L'Engle, *The Twelve and the Genii* by Pauline Clarke and *Mr Rabbit and the Lovely Present* by Charlotte Zolotow and illustrated by Maurice Sendak. The last of these shares the gently surreal traits of much of William Mayne's work. He himself said of his books, 'All I am doing is looking at things now and showing them to myself when young.' *The Twelve Dancers* is set in a Welsh village and centres on the search for a long-lost cup, a schoolteacher's gentle romance and the performance of a traditional dance by children around ancient standing stones.

William Mayne was probably at the height of his fame at the time of its publication, having won the prestigious Carnegie Medal in 1957, and a regular at Puffin Post events. He was, for many years, widely regarded as one of the best children's authors of the twentieth century and was as popular, if not more, with adults as younger readers. However, Mayne (1928–2010) and his work have largely been erased since he served two years in prison following his conviction in 2004 for several indecent assaults on young girls. Let's be absolutely clear – he pleaded guilty and was banned from contact with children indefinitely and put on the sex offenders register for the rest of his life. It's not hard to see why publishers and libraries have not exactly been queuing up to be associated with him in the twenty-first century.

The debate about how closely we associate creators with their work and whether we can continue to engage with what they have produced when it emerges that they have committed a crime is a thorny one. I would entirely understand if you feel unable or unwilling to read this book, but it's undeniably true that Mayne was a remarkably talented writer. He's probably best known today for his eerie time-slip story *Earthfasts*, which was made into a successful television series in 1994, and his quartet of boy chorister stories, which began with *A Swarm in May*. Like many of these books, *The Twelve Dancers* revolves around uncovering an old mystery – it's arguably a grail quest – and has a very strong evocation of landscape as well as an imaginative child's eye interpretation of the world. This is clear from the opening paragraph:

> Blue is the colour of the sky. Marlene was in bed still when she thought that. It was the colour of the sky in a chalk drawing or a painted drawing, but it was not the colour of the sky this morning. The sky now was green over the hills, with silver clouds lying untarnished above it. Higher still the sky was bruised with overhanging morning.

Mayne was born and lived most of his life in Yorkshire and regional dialect plays a strong part in many of his books in creating an atmospheric sense of place, coupled with down to earth realism. *The Twelve Dancers* is written in English but mirrors the Welsh language and uses Welsh syntax in an attempt to strengthen the flavour of Wales.

Though there is a (meandering) plot, it would be overstating it to say there's not much tension. Revelations are unearthed leisurely, and there's no traditional hero. Instead, it's Mayne's intense writing technique that really sets him apart. His very spare prose feels quite dreamlike, almost like we're reading or observing through a light gauze, even though nothing unfathomable happens. The book is mystical rather than magical realism. If it doesn't sound overly academic, there's a distinct whiff of Brechtian alienation about it because the reader is somehow distanced from the characters and action. Reading Mayne is a very hard experience to describe. He is somewhere between an encounter with Alan Garner (himself midway between *The Weirdstone of Brisingamen* and *The Moon of Gomrath* in 1962) and one with Enid Blyton (still knocking out her *Famous Five* adventures at this time). It's all about the journey, not the destination.

I find Mayne the man's actions entirely inexcusable, but, at the same time, I find that Mayne the writer's work is quite mesmerising.

Here's the final paragraph of this book:

> 'When I have a garden,' said Ma, 'I think I will only have a shrubbery of clouds. But for the most part it will be a big lawn of sky like this, and a dandelion of a sun; but I will never pull it up.'

The Twelve Dancers is certainly not a 'must read' but if you feel that a book can speak for itself rather than its author, then you'll discover a uniquely distinctive literary voice.

Why this book matters... the style is unlike any other kind of children's writer.

Read it because... Lynton Lamb's illustrations are a perfect fit for the text.

Give it a miss if... you understandably find it impossible to read bearing in mind Mayne's actions and criminal conviction.

What I discovered about Wales... it seems strangely very like Yorkshire...

BOOK 17

THE THOUGHTS
OF AN ISLANDER

◆

Tide-race
by Brenda Chamberlain
(1962)

This is a variation on the 'incomer' memoir, but one that makes
I Bought a Mountain look like Peter Mayle's 1989 inspirationally
matey bestselling effort about moving to France, *A Year in
Provence*.

This is writer and artist Brenda Chamberlain's account of living
on Ynys Enlli – in English, Bardsey Island – which is two miles
and a dangerous boat trip off the Llŷn Peninsula in northwest
Wales. Also known as the 'Island of 20,000 Saints', it has a long
history of religious activity, as well as being one of the many
alleged final resting places of Merlin the wizard of Arthurian
legend, and it is *extremely* remote. At its population peak, it only
had a couple of hundred residents, and by the time the newly
divorced Chamberlain arrived with her companion Jean Van de
Bijl (who becomes 'Paul' in the book), it was more like a dozen.
Today, it's down to half that.

Tide-race is considerably more complex than a simple
travelogue. Chamberlain (1912–71) was Welsh – though not
Welsh-speaking – and was born in Bangor. She married John

Petts, who published Alun Lewis's *Raider's Dawn*. Her line drawings pepper the text, and the first edition featured her abstract painting 'The Eye of the Sea' on the front cover, giving it the feel of an artist's book. There is also myth, legend, folktales and poetry in here. Dr Francesca Brooks has argued convincingly in her study 'From Blodeuwedd to The Wife's Lament: Medieval Remains in Brenda Chamberlain's Tide-race' that Chamberlain was inspired by medieval literature. The book certainly has a very Beowulfian beginning: 'LISTEN: I have found the home of my heart.'

The list of the permanent residents at the start of the book reads like a cast list for a play, and, indeed, the final sentence of this section is 'On this small stage, this microcosm, in the middle of a scene, the shadow of death falls on the players.' Throughout, Chamberlain smudges the factual sides of her fifteen years on Bardsey, which started in 1947, with an exuberant dash of creative writing. While this makes for an intriguing read, it doesn't always pay off. And, while she technically never names the island, the effort she made to anonymise the identities of the real islanders was so rudimentary that it deceived nobody. Even though it's dedicated to 'My Neighbours On The Island', when the book was published, they took exception to her portrayal of them, and she was asked to leave. And not come back.

However you classify it (maybe as an early example of psychogeography?) *Tide-race* is not a cosy memoir. The sea is a constant and constantly changing backdrop and one that is unrelentingly threatening. The islanders themselves are divided by a longstanding feud. Life is hard and intense, especially for the women who seem to live there only really because their husbands want to. There doesn't seem to be much joy in evidence and, while Chamberlain celebrates some aspects of a life lived in the most spartan and penurious surroundings, it doesn't feel like she had a great time in the decade and a half she lived there. She certainly doesn't sugarcoat the experience of living somewhere with few home comforts. The book feels like an accurate experience of survival. It also feels miserable, worrying, and uncomfortably like *The Wicker Man* but without flushing toilets.

Dr Brooks notes in her article that Caradog Prichard described *Tide-race* in his review for the *Daily Telegraph* as an 'often larger-than-life record of inbred savagery and primitive austerity among a salt-crusted, wave-lashed little community'. Chamberlain herself calls the island a 'deluding scrap of rock and turf' towards the end of the book. It's not hard to see why the inhabitants might have felt a little peeved.

So, what was Chamberlain trying to do by writing this book? Exorcise personal demons? Take a stand on behalf of women in the face of the centuries of male domination of the island? Or simply present her honest artistic response to the island? 'You Who Are In The Traffic Of The World' runs the book's epigraph, 'Can You Guess The Thoughts Of An Islander?'. To be honest, I'm not sure she could do that herself if she really believed the close-knit community that helped her make a home on their island would be happy with this book.

Putting all this aside, there are two major things in *Tide-race*'s favour. It is never boring or predictable and every turn of the page brings something unexpected. On top of this, Chamberlain writes beautifully. Here are a couple of examples:

> The island wore a deceptive summer innocence
> like a flower garden in which a serpent lay asleep.

And another, which takes us on a whistlestop descriptive tour of Enlli:

> A rock shore; cliffs of mussel-blue shell. Wine-red, icy pink, pure white, yellow and green. The surf creamed at the foot of the coloured walls.

Colours evoked images, images evoked words. Wall of jasper, tower of quartzite. How can a common seacliff be a wall of jasper?

When she left Bardsey, Chamberlain didn't return back to the mainland but headed to the island of Hydra in Greece, where she wrote another book about her experience there, *The Rope of Vines*. 'How far can I bend before I break,' she wrote in that book, but could so easily have done so too in *Tide-race*, 'how much salt water covers my head before I drown?'

Why this book matters... it's a genre-busting travelogue about life on a unique island.

Read it because... it will make you count your blessings about home comforts, plus the drawings add an atmospheric something to the book.

Give it a miss if... you don't like books in which it's hard to tell what's fact and what's fiction.

What I discovered about Wales... the reality of Ynys Enlli beyond a friend's account of a couple of enjoyable, if slightly spartan, holidays there.

BOOK 18

IT'S ME, NOT YOU

◆

The Book of Three
(part one of
The Chronicles of Prydain)
by Lloyd Alexander
(1964)

In his *The Life of Samuel Johnson*, James Boswell records that, on the morning of Tuesday, 15 June 1784, the great man commented on the advice of a certain Reverend Herbert Croft to a former pupil that if you start a book, then you should always finish it.

> 'This is surely a strange advice,' harrumphed Johnson. 'You may as well resolve that whatever men you happen to get acquainted with, you are to keep to them for life. A book may be good for nothing; or there may be only one thing in it worth knowing; are we to read it all through?'

Until the mid-1990s, I was of the exact opposite opinion of my namesake. Inspired by Magnus Magnusson, my guiding maxim was 'I've started, so I'll finish.' Even when the going got rough, I reminded myself that I had chosen – and indeed often shelled out hard cash for – this book and, by Jiminy, I was going to get my full money's worth. I believed that, once the spark had already been lit, it was my duty to the author and to my own self-esteem that I see it through to the bitter end.

Then I bought *The Age of Wire and String* by Ben Marcus in the excellent but sadly long-gone Bolingbroke Bookshop on Northcote Road in Clapham. 'An extraordinary first novel,' had said the *Times Literary Supplement*. 'Anticipates a career devoted to intelligent exploration of major themes,' foretold the *Chicago Tribune*. Yet, after about fifty pages and, with the heaviest of hearts, I decided the book wasn't for me. It wasn't Marcus's fault and it wasn't my fault – it just felt like I was trying to jam the wrong jigsaw piece into a hole.

Since then, there have been other books I have not finished. I'm not alone. In 2014, maths professor Jordan Ellenberg came up with the Hawking Index: a way of calibrating which books people gave up on most frequently based on how close to the end of the book they highlighted a passage on their Kindles. Top of the list of unfinished reads was *Hard Choices* by Hillary Clinton, and Stephen Hawking's *A Brief History of Time* was third. Conversely, his research suggested that 98.5 per cent of people finished *The Goldfinch* by Donna Tartt.

My personal list of non-finishers is quite short. Proust's *À la recherche du temps perdu* (In Search of Lost Time) is a recidivist entry (I've got to the end of *Swann's Way* (the first volume) twice, including once in French, and felt absolutely no desire to go any further). Sometimes, I've not given up completely. *Moby-Dick* was beyond me on several occasions over several years until I powered on through on the advice of a friend (thanks, Chris) and I am very glad that I did since I enjoyed it hugely. But still, there are a number of books out there that I haven't finished.

I didn't finish *The Book of Three*.

As with *The Age of Wire and String*, it's not that I thought it was a terrible book. If I thought that, I wouldn't have included it here at all. But, even though it seems to be universally popular, the winner of significant awards like the Newbery Medal and the basis for a Disney animated film, it just didn't click with me.

The Book of Three is the first in the series of five volumes that make up *The Chronicles of Prydain*. The title is a play on *Prydein* which is the medieval Welsh word for the island that is Britain. Lloyd Alexander was inspired by his time serving in Wales during the Second World War to create this semi-fantasy island. In his author's note, he's at pains to say it's not 'a retelling or retranslation of Welsh mythology' but he does acknowledge the debt it has to elements of the *Mabinogion*.

Aimed towards the younger end of the Young Adult category, what I've read of the book lays out the story of Taran, a slightly mardy teenager who is an assistant pig-keeper. Taran is very keen to become a famous hero but doesn't seem to have quite the requisite attributes. He teams up with someone who has distinct overtones of Tolkien's Aragorn and Princess Eilonwy, who is delightfully free of any fairy tale archetypes (for me, she was the most interesting character), as well as a Gollum-like creature, Gurgi, and a regal bard with distinct Cacofonix-from-*Asterix* vibes. Together, they battle against a mighty horned warlord. Imagine Frodo in Narnia rather than the Pevensie children in Middle-earth. If I'm making it sound a little derivative, I'm sure it's only because Alexander was drawing on the same mountain of legend that many other fantasy writers have mined, and, for many in the early 1960s, his work was a sparklingly new approach.

Admittedly, I'm not a voracious reader of fantasy these days. I was at thirteen and remain, at fifty-five, a very enthusiastic aficionado of *The Hobbit* and *The Lord of the Rings*, but other than the occasional dip into the genre over the intervening decades, that's about it. It's perhaps an unfair criticism of *The Book of Three*, but it strikes me as lacking the gravitas of a writer like Ursula K. Le Guin with her *Earthsea* novels (which I very much enjoyed) but, fair enough, not every schoolchild wants such solemn fare. Neither does it have the invention of Neil

Gaiman's *Stardust*. That said, I think children who are starting to enjoy something a bit more grown-up, such as Cornelia Funke's *Inkheart* series, and putting things like longstanding Wales resident Jenny Nimmo's *Charlie Bone* adventures behind them might get into it pretty quickly. And I don't see why adults wouldn't like it either – like a Pixar film, there is plenty there for the more mature reader to enjoy, too. Just not me.

Don't let me put you off though. Maybe this book caught me on a grumpy day. It might click with you. Not finishing a book isn't a defeat because reading is not a competition to the death. And I haven't given up completely on *The Book of Three*. I've reshelved it rather than releasing it back into the wild. But I do pinky promise that I'm not going to give up on any more on the Welshly list. Unless they feature any more magic pigs.

Why this book matters... according to the front cover of my copy, Garth Nix regards the author as 'the true High King of fantasy'.

Read it because... Princess Eilonwy, the real star of the show, takes no nonsense from anybody.

Give it a miss if... the idea of a Horned King running amok makes you yawn.

What I discovered about Wales... the said Horned King rules the territory of Annuvin, which comes from the old Welsh name Annwyn for the otherworld.

BOOK 19
FLOWERS NOT BIRDS
◆
The Owl Service
by Alan Garner
(1967)

From one that I didn't finish reading to one that I've read twice.

Rereading is quite different from reading, like watching a repeat on television that is somehow different. The first frisson of the original encounter is missing, but I've often found that's more than made up for a) by not having to concentrate on remembering exactly who everybody is and b) understanding it a lot better, whether that's by noticing important details or just bringing a new perspective to the text. And there's perhaps a slight element of guilt for me since, every time I read a book a second time, it means I'm not reading somebody else's book even once – but I get over my remorse pretty quickly.

Plenty of big names have given the act of rereading the thumbs up. That fine essayist William Hazlitt wrote in his 1821 article 'On Reading Old Books' that, 'I hate to read new books. There are twenty or thirty volumes that I have read over and over again, and these are the only ones that I have any desire to ever read at all.' His argument was that, in rereading, he knew what to expect and that, in no way, lessened his satisfaction. Indeed, it actually *added* to the pleasure because of the memories associated with the first time of asking. *Lonesome Dove* writer and bibliophile Larry McMurtry expressed similar opinions once he'd reached his eighth decade of life: 'I now read for security. How nice to be able to return to what won't change.'

What I find odd is that I have several friends who quite happily watch the same treasured film numerous times and seem to play the same records and CDs on repeat but, even though they keep plenty of books, never reread any of them. If you go somewhere fabulous on holiday, there's no shame in going back, is there? If I can't convince you about the benefits of rereading then track down a copy of Anne Fadiman's 2006 book *Seventeen Writers Revisit Books They Love*, which is splendid.

In the case of *The Owl Service*, what a difference several decades make. I first read it in my late teens when I had the Armada Lions edition which is one of the least creepy of all the available versions. The cover shows just Alison (one of the three lead teenage characters) looking a bit Ophelia-like and holding a bunch of flowers with an owl-ish dinner plate in the background. That may sound actually quite weird, but it's nothing compared to the 1967 first edition design by Kenneth Farnhill, which has a kind of writhing Medusa tangle of roots that, in my view, is more than somewhat unsettling.

I recall enjoying the book, but that's about all I can remember. The Welshness, which absolutely dominates every page of the book, I'm ashamed to say, made absolutely no impact on me at all at age thirteen. It's all the more a blot in my copybook because Garner, a devotee of Ordnance Survey maps, pays minute attention to detail to achieve this sense of place. I remember a BBC Radio 4 programme in which he walked around his signature location of Alderley Edge and pointed out to the presenter, Clare Balding, the exact root on which his fictitious heroine Susan trips over in the first book, *The Weirdstone of Brisingamen*. In *The Owl Service*, the setting is the very real Welsh settlement of Llanymawddwy, where he visited and spent time talking to the local population. He even learned

Welsh, not in order to write in it, but to make sure his written dialogue, which is in English, still felt authentic.

And so, several years of research resulted in this story of three teenagers who find themselves trapped in a kind of living *Mabinogion* – the book which is increasingly popping up everywhere as the Welshly list unravels. English teen step-siblings Roger and Alison are on holiday with their parents in a house previously owned by Alison's dead father. Looking after them – if that's quite the right term for their unimpressive parenting styles – are Welsh housekeeper Nancy and her son Gwyn. The teens discover a dinner service in the attic – the original 1880s plate that partly inspired the book is in the collection of The Story Museum in Oxford – and find themselves unwillingly drawn into what appears to be the ongoing recreation of a key story in the *Mabinogion*: that of Blodeuwedd, her husband Lleu, and a second man, Gronw.

The Owl Service is interesting on so many levels. This is the first book where accidentally including major spoilers here would not be an issue because simply revealing what happens on the final pages would make no sense unless you'd read the previous 200. And, to be honest, even if you have read the previous 200, it's still all up for discussion. The author is not keen to explain. He wants the reader to think it through themselves, which I think we can all agree is a good thing.

The Owl Service is largely marketed as a YA book and there is a decidedly overpowering whiff of hormones in the action, but Garner has repeatedly said that he's writing for himself, not a particular age group or market. Like me, I think it's one of those books that you can get plenty out of reading and then rereading at different times of life. There's an older generation involved in the story, too, so perhaps in another decade, I should give it another shake and see what emerges.

Although Garner writes very sparsely, the book ranges over many issues: English property ownership in Wales; class; how the past and 'legend' influences the present; the profound impact of certain locations on human life; varying cultural approaches to speaking Welsh versus English; and motherhood. It's also sometimes described as fantasy. Garner has rather distanced himself from this analysis. As he wrote in his excellent collection of essays, *A Voice That Thunders*, 'far from being escapist, fantasy is an intensification of reality.' Instead, he has pointed to the inspiration of the *Mabinogion* as 'such a modern story of the damage people do to each other, not through evil in themselves, but through the unhappy combination of circumstance that throws otherwise harmless personalities together.' It's also a very good summing up of *The Owl Service*. It is quite a claustrophobic book, one that Garner has called 'a kind of ghost story' and one that, second time around, I found pretty terrifying.

Why this book matters... it's a gripping depiction of the angst of adolescence.

Read it because... it's another key in the lock to getting to grips with the *Mabinogion*.

Give it a miss if... you want an ending that ties all the loose ends up nice and neatly.

What I discovered about Wales... reservoir construction has been a hugely contentious issue.

BOOK 20

A WORLD OF HIGH ADVENTURE!

◆

The Shop in the Mountain
by *Showell Styles*
(1968)

While it's something of a challenge – albeit a pleasant one – deciding which book to read next as an adult, when I was a nipper, I had no such problems. Rather than overthinking whether I'd read enough poetry this month or too many books by men over the course of the year, I simply read whatever I came across or was put in my hands. So at about the same time that I read *The Nose Knows* by E. W. Hildick (pre-teen friends start a detection club based largely on one of the member's amazing sense of smell), I also collided with *The Brothers Karamazov* (suggested to me by my father and I can't remember a thing about it now). In retrospect, this haphazard approach could have been refined if I'd paid any attention whatsoever to the reading age suggestions. At the time, I didn't realise they even existed.

The Shop in the Mountain by Showell Styles is, in my 1968 Atlantic Press edition, marked for readers aged twelve to fifteen. That means it falls into the publisher's Green Dragon series (which eclectically includes *My Friend Flicka* by Mary O'Hara, *Beau Geste* by P. C. Wren, *Tarzan of the Apes* by Edgar

Rice Burroughs and *Doctor Who and the Crusaders* by David Whitaker) as opposed to the Red Dragons, aimed at the age group below (the *Malory Towers* and the *St Clare's* series by Enid Blyton and R. M. Ballantyne's antidote to William Golding's *Lord of the Flies*, *The Coral Island*).

The Shop in the Mountain was recommended to me by a friend who said he thought he liked it when he read it forty years ago – which is good enough for me. And the book is *The Railway Children* meets the *Famous Five* up a Welsh mountain. Caroline, a mother and a widow since her husband died in questionable circumstances in a climbing accident in Nepal, and her three young children, Simon, Margaret or Mag, and Dilys or Dilly, are forced by economic necessity to up sticks. They leave their Surrey home and head to a mountain village in Wales not far from Porthmadog and a tiny cottage that was previously owned by the children's Welsh grandpa. Here, they set up the shop of the title. The village, Nant, is fictitious, but the text reveals it's not far from the very real village of Garreg.

A key attraction of their new home, for Simon at least, is that it is surrounded by mountains and, although his mother makes him promise not to go clambering around them, well... Here's the blurb:

> High in the rough, lonely hills of North Wales Simon, Mag and Dilly Hughes find adventure they never dreamed of. Simon wins his climbing boots one storm-washed night by saving an inexperienced hiker lying injured in the treacherous crags. Mag and Dilly also discover the camp of a Roman legion made centuries before. With the speed of a mountain avalanche this story sweeps you into a world of high adventure!

The book also delightedly exclaims that this is 'The first of an exciting mountaineering series about Mag and Simon Hughes'.

Although this is true, and it was followed by three more, this first volume is very much focused on the fourteen-year-old Simon rather than eleven-year-old Mag. Perhaps this was an admirable attempt by the publishers to encourage girls to give the book a go. Mag is, however, at the centre of one of the strangest episodes in the book. She bangs her head and has the kind of mystical experience that Ratty and Mole have in chapter seven of *The Wind in the Willows*, 'The Piper at the Gates of Dawn'.

Simon is another incomer to Wales, and his journey is a very relevant one. At the start, he's very proud of being English and, although he likes his new home, he's keen on preserving his Englishness. He refuses to learn Welsh, even though his sisters are keen to learn the new language. But by the end of the story, he has very much changed his tune. In fact, if you don't know any Welsh, you will have to look up a translation of the last words of the book, which are Simon's response to a question asking him what he thinks of a major change in the family situation. This rather mirrors the author's own experience. Frank Showell Styles (1908–2005) came from Birmingham but learned the ropes of mountaineering as a child in Wales before he became a naval officer and then a writer. He wrote a bit for *Punch* magazine but then turned his hand to books, producing around 160 for both children and adults, including travel guides. When he retired, he moved to Borth-y-Gest and then to Croesor (where he, too, ran a shop), both near Porthmadog. Throughout his life, he loved walking and climbing in Wales. Consequently, there's a lot of mountaineering in the book. I acknowledge that somebody with a greater interest than me in farming would get much more out of *I Bought a Mountain*, so if climbing is your thing, then there is plenty here that probably went over my head (or that I whizzed through a bit swiftly) and will appeal more to you.

I don't intend to read the others in the series *The Ladder of Snow* (1962), *A Necklace of Glaciers* (1963) and *The Pass of Morning* (1966), although I do like the sound of another of

Styles's creations. Sir Abercrombie 'Filthy' Lewker, the hero of another of his series, is an actor and – *quelle surprise* – mountaineer who sometimes solves murders at high altitude in Wales. Another gem I discovered while rummaging about in Styles's past was a monologue he wrote about climbing in Wales called *The Ballad of Idwal Slabs*. He wrote it in much the same kind of style as Marriott Edgar's *The Lion and Albert* monologue for actor Stanley Holloway. *The Battle of Idwal Slabs* hinges on a life-saving chance in a million, which involves catching the braces of a mountaineer's trousers on a rock. Comedy gold.

Why this book matters... it's a jolly romp with – and I don't think this counts as a spoiler as you'll see it coming well in advance – a happy ending.

Read it because... it is brilliantly encouraging about the positive effects of learning Welsh.

Give it a miss if... you want to avoid extended scenes of hunting foxes.

What I discovered about Wales... King Arthur threw Excalibur into the Llyn Llydaw lake in Eryri (Snowdonia). Allegedly.

BOOK 21

A WOMAN'S NOVEL, A MAN'S NOVEL

◆

Travels with a Duchess
by *Menna Gallie*
(1968)

If there's anything the media loves more than a shortcut, it's a reusable shortcut. If you search 'real life Shirley Valentine' online, you'll get hundreds of results. Willy Russell's creation, the title character of his 1986 one-character play *Shirley Valentine*, has become headline writers' common shorthand for middle-aged women whose lives are transformed by a holiday abroad.

I'm absolutely not accusing Russell of pinching Gallie's plot, not least because when he wrote his play, her 1968 novel was even less well known than it is now, despite publishing house Honno's fine work in republishing it in 1996 (my copy is a 2011 reprint). But still, *Travels with a Duchess* is absolutely Shirley Valentine *avant la lettre*.

Shirley— sorry! Innes is a respectable fortysomething Cardiff schoolteacher whose holiday plans for a trip to Yugoslavia with her dentist husband hit the rocks when he has to attend a conference in Coventry at the last minute. Encouraged by him, she heads off alone, teaming up en route with a Catholic woman from Northern Ireland (the 'Duchess' of the title) who is also by herself as her husband and children are back in the family home. Together and away from the confines of home, they have a rather liberating experience.

While it would give the wrong impression to call *Travels with a Duchess* a 'sex caper' or another lazy shortcut like 'women behaving badly', there is a lot about sexuality in it. 'This is a terrible chronicle of debauchery,' says Innes directly to the reader. 'It is by my standards anyway because I'm a very typical, ordinary, middle-class wife.' All the men seem to have one-track minds, and there's an episode of voyeurism which, mark my words, will have you going 'yuck' and making a face. As historian and biographer Professor Angela V. John says in the foreword, this is a novel that is 'luxuriating in its frankness'.

John also calls it 'a woman's novel', a description that also makes it to the blurb on the back cover. To be honest, I'm not exactly sure what a 'woman's novel' is. Clare Hanson, in her book *Hysterical Fictions: The 'Woman's Novel' in the Twentieth Century*, offers this definition: 'fiction which, while immensely popular among educated women readers, sits uneasily between high and low culture'. In a marvellous 1986 piece for *Ms* magazine, 'What Is a Woman's Novel? For That Matter, What Is a Man's?', Margaret Atwood suggests that: 'Men's novels are about men. Women's novels are about men, too, but from a different point of view. You can have a men's novel with no women in it, except possibly the landlady or the horse, but you can't have a women's novel with no men in it.' The cover of the 1968 first edition of *Travels with a Duchess* hedged its bets on its key readership, suggesting that it was 'A sparklingly gay fairy tale for wives (and husbands): a novel that explores every woman's dream of romantic independence'.

The book was partly inspired by Gallie's own trip, in 1965, to a PEN (Poets, Essayists, Novelists) International conference in Dubrovnik. The focus of the story is certainly on women's experiences of travelling. Innes is almost stopped from flying because her passport states that a wife may not travel alone on a joint passport without her husband's consent (I know!). She later has a brush with a local policeman over a joke telegram.

It would be a shame if men were put off from reading this or encouraged to dismiss it offhand as 'chick lit' or similar. Gallie is a marvellous writer and while this, at first, appears to be quite a slim volume, its message – that a #MeToo-type campaign in 1968 was already somewhat overdue – is still potent.

It's also very funny, especially the parts that centre on Welshness. At one point, Innes improvises the Lord's Prayer in Welsh for an academic purely so he can hear how it sounds. But she forgets the words halfway through and has to improvise by adding in bits of modern poetry. Innes has a very robust attitude to her country and, later in the book, at a dinner party notes that she was 'putting on a kind of Gwyn Thomas tour de force and talking about Wales as if it really bore some relation to *How Green Was My Valley*, a book they thought much of.' She even offers a term to describe it, 'walocs': 'a mixture of affectation, pretentiousness, posing, whimsy, would-be-ness, making a performance, a parade of notions, of sentimentalities ... the opposite of plain common sense, bitter realities, simplicities, honesties.'

Innes is, in her own undemanding way, a force to be reckoned with, as was her character Cynthia in *The Small Mine*. If you liked Shirley Valentine, and you're a woman – or a man or anybody with a sense of humour – I guarantee you will like this.

Why this book matters... it shows, without being preachy, the injustices of misogyny that women battle against.

Read it because... it's great fun.

Give it a miss if... you're one of those people who 'can't see what women have against a bit of banter'.

What I discovered about Wales... it can be quite racy.

BOOK 22

MUCK AND GLORY

♦

So Long, Hector Bebb
by Ron Berry
(1970)

If *Travels with a Duchess* really is a woman's book, then it could be argued that *So Long, Hector Bebb* – the story of a young boxer from Cymmer, south Wales – is a man's.

This is not a novel garlanded lusciously with purple prose. If, like Menna Gallie's Innes, you found *How Green Was My Valley* a bit on the sentimental side, then this is your gritty antidote: a down-to-earth work that plays with words and speech. It is something of a counterpart to Dylan Thomas's monologues in *Under Milk Wood* and a forerunner to Irvine Welsh's *Trainspotting*. I remember one of my sons turning to me as we finished watching the film *Stand By Me* and saying how amazing it was that the dialogue so closely matched how he and his friends talked at school. I'm sure this is the feeling that many people must also feel when reading *So Long, Hector Bebb* for the first time. Although, it should also be said that if you are offended by sex references, this is not the book for you.

The chronicle of the rise and fall of the young and very masculine Hector Bebb is told by fourteen different key characters in the novel. It's really quite gripping and, in fact, it's arguably a kind of thriller. At the start of the book, Bebb is planning a boxing comeback after a year's break following a fight that ended unpleasantly for all concerned, especially for his opponent. Bebb is pretty sure of himself, but the Greek chorus around him is generally not so much. Unfortunately for Hector, the Cassandras are bang on the mark. We're not in the upbeat country of the *Rocky* movies here (well, perhaps the early part of the first film is to some extent) because Berry is exploring a far more sophisticated place. Hector is not set up as any kind of hero or, indeed, as an anti-hero. Berry – who was himself a keen and accomplished sportsman – does not sit in judgement on him and his actions. 'We're each and every one of us shaped for muck and glory,' says Sammy, Hector's trainer.

What starts off as a boxing story about a boy who makes good after a rotten early start in life, turns into an exploration of how a working-class community of boxers, managers, trainers and their wives and girlfriends constantly circle each other. Berry concentrates on these brutal lives orbiting the unwitting Bebb and their relationships with him. One of the most interesting of these is the relationship Bebb has with local landowner Prince Jenkin Saddler. He is a war veteran who has lost an arm in combat and appears to suffer from depression. He has a long-term fiancée, but it is his friendship with Bebb that energises him. In a novel full of heterosexual relationships – marital and extra-marital – Prince is an anomaly in that he is obviously strongly attracted to Hector, both physically and also for what he stands for as a fighter. He tries to keep his feelings hidden from himself as much as anybody else, but his fiancée is not fooled.

So Long, Hector Bebb is also the first book on my list where it doesn't feel the author has deliberately written about a Welsh woman or man, a Welsh place, or a specifically Welsh issue. Berry has written a story first, and it happens to be set in Wales.

Berry (1920–97) did not have a straightforward literary career. Born in Blaencwm in the upper Rhondda valley, he fought in the Second World War and also worked as a miner and carpenter.

So Long, Hector Bebb was his fifth novel and, though he produced more short stories and some well-regarded nature writing, his star unfairly rather withered away. Many of the books on the Welshly list are now reaching a wider audience thanks to determined independent publishers who believe in them. *So Long, Hector Bebb* has had a helping hand to lift it up from the Library of Wales project by the Welsh Assembly, which aims to promote the literature of Wales in English internationally. In a note at the end of my 2006 edition, series editor Dai Smith describes their ongoing publishing mission as 'a key component in creating and disseminating an ongoing sense of modern Welsh culture and history for the future Wales which is now emerging from contemporary society'.

It's only tangentially related but, just after I finished *So Long Hector Bebb*, I found out that the early twentieth century Welsh world lightweight boxing champion Freddie Welsh, who was born in Pontypridd, may have been the model for Jay Gatsby in F. Scott Fitzgerald's *The Great Gatsby*. Apparently, he and Fitzgerald did a bit of sparring. It's a funny old world – and one in which the influence of Wales and the Welsh on the wider world should never be underestimated.

Why this book matters... it plays around inventively with structure without being overly tricksy.

Read it because... the dialogue is particularly well done.

Give it a miss if... you object to strong language.

What I discovered about Wales... it makes a fine background for modern as well as ancient myth stories.

BOOK 23

A CHILDREN'S BOOK FOR ADULTS

♦

Carrie's War
by Nina Bawden
(1973)

A few years ago I started keeping a list of books I'd read so that I could keep some kind of track of them. When I consult this list, it tells me that, early in 2018, I was struggling through *List of the Lost* by Morrissey. Two years later, I was whizzing through Anthony Buckeridge's *Jennings and the Unconsidered Trifles*. Then, in the summer of 2022, I was sampling Leonie Rushforth's poetry collection *Deltas*.

I wish I'd started my list sooner because there are some books – and by some, I mean *lots* – which I *think* I've read, but I'm just not sure. So, I've definitely read *Midnight's Children* by Salman Rushdie. There it is on my bookshelf, fenced in by *Nobody's Fool* by Richard Russo and Arundhati Roy's *The God of Small Things*. I remember buying it new when it was all lovely and shiny and unread, from a bookshop (Godfreys in York, sadly no longer with us). And there it is now – having been through the wars, shoddily glued spine broken, loose pages held in place with a rubber band around its middle, a couple of corners turned down, a faint coffee ring on its back cover. It looks a bit like a prop in a film, so deliberately has it been embellished with the marks of having been read. But I can't recall a thing about *Midnight's Children*. Not a character's name, any incidents, or how it starts or how it ends. Nothing.

But *Nobody's Fool*, there's one I've *definitely* read. My wife gave it to me for my birthday. And yes, I can tell you the names of at least three characters, I can give you a vaguely accurate precis of the plot and I know how it finishes. It's all in my head. Yet my copy of *Nobody's Fool* looks absolutely pristine. I'm *sure* I've read it... but now I'm a bit suspicious that I just watched (and enjoyed) the film of the book starring Paul Newman as Sully.

And, technically, I *have* read Emily Brontë's *Wuthering Heights*. During the summer holidays when I was eleven and casting around for something to get stuck into, I picked it up at random from my parents' bookcase. I say I 'read' it but, looking back, all I really did was look at all the words. I didn't understand what was going on. So, I'm not sure it really counts.

So, when I added *Carrie's War* to the Welshly list, I was sure I'd read it and that I had enjoyed it, so I looked forward to immersing myself again in it. But, in fact, I found nothing about it was at all familiar and now suspect that I got no further than the blurb all those many moons ago. I wish I *had* read it 'back then' because, not only is it an excellent book, it's one of those that a child and an adult reads with very different eyes. Events shift in their significance according to the age of a reader. Although written for children, perhaps it has become such a popular book to reread for adults because this is actually a story about adults and not children.

Eleven-year-old Carrie and her nine-year-old brother Nick are evacuated, as Bawden herself was, from London during the Second World War to a small Welsh village. They are assigned to live with an elderly grizzly bear of a grocer, Mr Evans, and his put-upon sister, Auntie Lou. Another evacuee, the fabulously named, Albert Sandwich, is staying with the Evanses' sister and her cousin, Johnny, who has cerebral palsy, in the nearby house Druid's Bottom. Here, the housekeeper, Hepzibah Green, is known as a wise woman and acts as a counter to Mr Evans's uncompromising chapel-inspired lifestyle. We follow how the evacuees change the lives of the adults around them until the fateful final day when Carrie and Nick leave.

It's not really a coming-of-age tale, but Carrie's feelings as she tries her best to understand the actions of the adults around her, including the seemingly less likeable ones, show she is caught between the innocence of her younger brother and the more complex ambiguities of grown-up life. Albert and Carrie both feel that childhood renders them powerless but, in fact, the children have a far bigger impact on the lives around them in *Carrie's War* than they imagine. In *Carrie's War* we're not a million miles from *Swallows and Amazons* territory, but with a dash of *Jane Eyre*, too.

Like *Wuthering Heights*, it's also a frame story (yes, I looked at those words again as a twentysomething and found I understood them). The book starts with a grown-up and newly widowed Carrie visiting the Welsh town, with her own young children, thirty years after she and Nick left, and it ends with her children going on their own parallel pilgrimage to Druid's Bottom.

It's rightly become a favourite in schools because, as well as a springboard from which to discuss evacuation and war, it also raises issues about bullying, relationships, class and English colonialism in Wales. There's also an important strand of the story which references the slave trade, an echo of which is recounted in the scene where Carrie and Nick endure what Albert describes as a 'cattle auction' upon their arrival in Wales when they are picked for their new homes.

But there is so much here for adults, too. While the major part of the action is presented through the young Carrie's eyes, the framing elements are told with the wisdom of her older self so it turns into a book about growing up and making sense of childhood. Intriguingly, Carrie's and Nick's middle names are Wendy and Peter... Is Bawden perhaps suggesting that the experience of war forced children to grow up as opposed to staying childlike like Peter Pan?

Carrie's War is also a book about belief and how it affects our lives. For good or bad, Mr Evans leans as heavily on his Christianity as Hepzibah does on her 'old religion'. When Carrie's eldest boy pooh-poohs any credence in druids as foolish, his mother replies, 'There's always a reason for legends.' It's certainly also about a belief in place. At the start of the book, the adult Carrie is still trying to make sense of her life. 'Places change more than people, perhaps,' she tells her children. 'You don't change, you know, growing older.' Maybe, maybe not, but Carrie is undoubtedly linked to this landscape. Over the intervening years since she left, she has dreamed regularly about returning and feels a particularly strong connection to the grove, a strange woody area between Mr Evans's home and Druid's Bottom. This is where she had a mystical experience as a child.

> Deep in the trees or deep in the earth ... something
> old and huge and nameless ... a slow, dry whisper,
> or sigh. As if the earth was turning in its sleep.

She can't explain what she hears in this moment, but Albert has a shot at it: 'I think it's just that places where people have believed things have an odd feel to them.'

Why this book matters... it's perhaps the best novel about the wartime evacuation of children.

Read it because... it shows what happens if you let family feuds develop over time.

Give it a miss if... you don't agree with Hamlet that 'There are more things in Heaven and Earth, Horatio, than are dreamt of in your philosophy.'

What I discovered about Wales... evacuees from London didn't just end up in rural England.

BOOK 24

THE TOP LEFT-HAND CORNER

◆

Ivor the Engine – Snowdrifts
by Oliver Postgate and Peter Firmin
(1977)

'What is the use of a book,' Alice, quite rightly, asks herself right at the start of her adventures in Wonderland, 'without pictures or conversation?' It would be a sorry reading list that couldn't make room for at least one picture book (if you would prefer a book with pictures, I'd recommend Dylan Thomas's *A Child's Christmas in Wales* in the editions with drawings by the incomparable Edward Ardizzone or, more recently, by Peter Bailey).

I was initially a bit unsure if the list should include Ivor the Engine, arguably the best-known Welsh personality of the twentieth century outside the country. His mild bassoon-fuelled jaunts at The Merioneth and Llantisilly Rail Traction Company Limited located in the top left-hand corner of Wales, have been the soundtrack to generations of television viewers, so it seemed somewhat redundant to include them here. However, while I found the *Noggin the Nog* books – his stablemate at the Postgate and Firmin Small Films production setup – absolutely enthralling, I never actually read any *Ivor the Engine* books as a child. In fact, I didn't even know they existed. So I closed my eyes, stuck a pin in a search engine and added *Snowdrifts* to the Welshly list. And I'm glad I did because there's far more to this thirty-two-page story than simply a charming little read with pretty drawings.

It's only slightly quicker to offer a swift precis than copy the whole book out, but the action is set in winter (not specifically Christmas time, though the general feel is undoubtedly Christmassy) in the town of Llaniog, where Ivor lives and works. It has been snowing so hard that supplies cannot get through to the local shopkeepers, who urge Ivor and his stalwart driver, Jones the Steam, to plough through the drifts to get through to nearby Grumbly Town and return with the goods. No spoilers, of course, but let's just say that the good burghers of Llaniog are not wanting for long in terms of (deep breath) 'flour, potatoes, carrots, sprouts, onions, leeks, bull's eyes, beef-cubes, camphor, combs, caraway seeds, detergents, dolly mixtures, embrocation, flannel nighties, grapefruit, hatpins, hair oil, honey and Miss Figgin's old uncle'.

As a nipper, Ivor always reminded me of the equally sentient vehicle Herbie the VW Beetle who, in the same year *Snowdrifts* came out, was in cinemas whizzing around Monte Carlo at a car rally. Both have a mind of their own and are fully up for larking around. Indeed, unlike the often-unlikeable Thomas the Tank Engine and his cohort, the less visually anthropomorphic Ivor operates in a much more relaxed organisation. Yes, there are a few rules and regulations, but when Jones and Dai Station (the stationmaster) first appear in the tale, the chaps have their feet up on the stove in the booking office and are drinking tea. Ivor is hanging out with some sheep friends who are warming themselves on his boiler. They are certainly not clockwatching jobsworths, maniacally ensuring that punctuality targets are met.

However, even though they appear technically off-timetable, Ivor is at the heart of his community and when that community calls for help, he wheels forward. The *Thomas* stories are about trains. *Snowdrifts*, like the other *Ivor* tales, is about humanity. While favourite characters from the television series, such as Mrs Porty and Idris the dragon, sadly do not put in an appearance in this particular story, the likes of Eli the Baker and Mrs Williams the Sweetshop are absolutely central. 'I didn't expect to see you again till after the snow!' says Mr Thomas, the stationmaster at Grumbly (who also has his feet up with a cuppa). 'Well, it's a bit of an emergency, like,' replies Jones. 'We can't let the town starve, can we?' Ivor's trainline appears to be run for the community good rather than for profit – an idea that shouldn't sound as groundbreaking as it does.

Ivor is no pushover, though. At one point, he refuses to steam through a snowdrift, despite Jones's growing impatience, because he's spotted sheep trapped within it and, when the shopkeepers get huffy because his love of animals causes a slight delay in the goods delivery, he gives them a massive POOOOOOOOP on his whistle to point out their selfishness. Ivor is kind and *Snowdrifts* underlines that he has a strong commitment to his civic duty.

Compared to many other of Ivor's adventures, there are fewer instances of the frequent Welsh stereotypes that Postgate deliberately drew on, such as mining, dragons and choirs. I'm speaking as an outsider here, of course, but my hot take is that Ivor is something of a love letter to the Welsh nation rather than a pantomime raspberry. In his autobiography, *Seeing Things*, Postgate admitted that he regularly carried a copy of *Under Milk Wood* around with him – indeed he even called a town in Ivor's world Llanmad, which is surely a homage to Dylan Thomas's Llareggub. And he also wrote: 'in my mind, Wales was already a magical place, a place of glorious eccentricities and unlikely logic'.

There's certainly a kind of understated magical realism involved in Ivor's world. Ivor is fully accepted by the local population without comment despite his obvious unusual characteristics making him an extraordinary member of an ordinary neighbourhood. It's a tolerant rather than a utopian society, but it does feel like one in which people are pulling together rather than being under the thumb of non-resident bosses. If Ivor is standing in for the young reader, the townsfolk do a fine job of co-parenting him. It, as they say, takes a village. And it's all very uplifting.

For an added bonus, you can even enjoy Oliver Postgate reading *Snowdrifts* to you online – just search on YouTube – which is a lovely twelve-minute treat, complete with a crackly old recording for added atmosphere. And, if you are in the mood for some literary detective work, you might also try to track down a copy of the only *Ivor the Engine* story in Welsh in existence. In 2009, Postgate's son Daniel wrote a new *Ivor* tale in a bilingual edition called *Bluebell's Christmas Mission/Cenhadaeth Nadolig Bluebell* with illustrations by Peter Firmin. This very short story of half a dozen pages tells the story of Bluebell the donkey helping deliver '*twrci, cracers a pwdin*' (I haven't actually looked these up in my Welsh-English dictionary, but I'm willing to bet a shiny pound coin on what these yuletide essentials are) to Mr Pugh's farm through heavy snowdrifts. The book was published to raise funds for animal charity SPANA, the Society for the Protection of Animals Abroad. Out of print for years, I failed to find a copy but someone with more perseverance might be more lucky.

Why this book matters... it emphasises the important things in life.

Read it because... Peter Firmin's illustrations are delightful.

Give it a miss if... you think only children should read children's books.

What I discovered about Wales... branch-line trains are vital rural lifelines.

BOOK 25

IMMANENT STRUCTURAL CONTRADICTIONS

◆

The Volunteers
by Raymond Williams
(1978)

Just because you like one book by an author, there's no reason you should like them all. I'm a huge fan of Garrison Keillor's *Lake Wobegon* books, but his other work leaves me chilly. Jeanette Winterson is also a game of two halves for me. I loved *Border Country*, and, pretty much on that basis alone, I added *The Volunteers* to the Welshly list. Unfortunately, this next book from Raymond Williams gets a no from me.

Williams sets the scene slightly in the future from his time of writing. We're in a bleak version of the late 1980s, not quite *Nineteen Eighty-Four* territory, but mildly evil corporations and unwholesomely large media giants are very much the order of the day. There's even some sci-fi gadgetry thrown into Williams's imagined world. In south Wales, where coalminers are on strike, one of their number is killed. A few months later, a government minister with possible links to the miner's death is also shot. Enter former radical and now hard-bitten journalist (is there any other kind?) Lewis Redfern to try and work out what's what and who's who as we are whirled away into a world of conspiracy theories, full of secret organisations and middle-class Wolfie Smith revolutionaries dressing down while they transfer power to the people.

I did not find this, as the blurb promised on my 2011 copy from the publisher, Parthian, a 'compelling thriller'. Though it does have an interesting foreword by outspoken former Labour MP Kim Howells, who worked both for the National Union of Mineworkers and later as chair of parliament's Intelligence and Security Committee. Howells loves the book. 'It is as if, in the critical years of the late 1970s, Williams is translating into fiction Lenin's warnings of the temptations, weaknesses and dangers of "infantile leftism", whether it took the form of isolated violence or industrial syndicalism.' This was the major problem for me. It felt too much like a working through of ideas and, while I have no problem with that, there was insufficient focus on characters, really creaky dialogue and shaky plotting that was more of an issue. 'The whole point about living in a society like this,' the character, Redfern, ponders to himself at one point, 'is that people get so confused by what our theoreticians call the immanent structural contradictions that they don't have to change, dramatically, in old soul-saving or soul-selling ways.' This might well be true, but there was far too much of this kind of writing to keep me interested. I can neither confirm nor deny that I occasionally mouthed 'Parklife' during this section of the reading journey.

Early on, Williams gives St Fagans National Museum of History, then known as the Welsh Folk Museum, a bit of a kicking for failing to represent the country's history fully, but he turns it into the kind of academic musing you might get from a senior don at Oxford during a tutorial, not always the most riveting of experiences. *The Volunteers* is novel as treatise. Increasingly, as the truth unravels, the permanently glum Redfern tussles with questions of morality and political loyalty, but he doesn't engage the reader on a personal level, and the writing can be so turgid at times that, however worthy the sentiments, it all feels a bit cold. Maybe if I were Welsh, or more working class, or was more involved with the nitty-gritty of politics, I would have felt differently. If you are, maybe you will get more out of this book than me. Then again, maybe not. In its favour, the book does have a cracking final line so, if you do decide to give it a go, then you have that to look forward to.

Why this book matters... it foreshadows some of the darker sides to life today that have developed thanks to modern media technology.

Read it because... it's a rare intellectual political thriller.

Give it a miss if... you don't like the feeling of being in a lecture hall.

What I discovered about Wales... St Fagans National Museum of History: which, despite Williams's reservations, sounds well worth a visit.

BOOK 26

THE WRONG BABY

◆

The Sundial
by *Gillian Clarke*
(1978)

I bought my copy of *The Sundial* from a second-hand bookshop. It has an arresting front cover featuring two leafless trees against a background of white hills and a bright sun high in a red sky so that it looks like the moon. The endorsements on the back cover include one from a fellow St Albans resident, the poet John Mole, who admires Clarke's exploration of the landscape of the Welsh hills and her ability to conjure memorable images. And, from the moment I opened it, I knew this poetry collection was going to be a keeper. Because it was signed by the author.

My day job is online editor for *Fine Books & Collections* magazine so I spend a decent portion of each day writing about rare books, manuscripts, maps, comics and related ephemera such as Ernest Hemingway's typewriter. But I still get a little buzz whenever I type the words 'signed copy' in an article. In monetary terms, it's obviously a marker of higher value (though I've signed so many of my own books that the unsigned ones are probably worth a bit more). Originally £1.50, similar signed copies are going for at least £15 at the moment. Not that I'm interested in the cash, you understand. For me, it's more than that – it's the feeling that the copy in your hands has passed through the hands of the author. The Cardiff-born Welsh poet Gillian Clarke has an attractive signature – legible but stylish – and has added 'with best wishes' to my copy, which is nice.

Clarke is not the only person who's written in my copy, which is the 1982 third impression. J. M. Hindley bought the book a little later, not only writing their name on the first page but also adding the date, 1984. This addition would appeal to writer and publisher Nicholas Royle who, in his book *Shadow Lines*, explains how his scouring of second-hand bookshops is partly motivated by the search for 'inclusions' – the odds and ends people leave behind in books, including inscriptions such as these. Royle has even tracked down some of the previous owners and offered to return their inscribed books to them for free. So far, I've had no luck finding J. M. Hindley, though I like to think it's the same person who gave the film *Sharkenstein* only two stars on Amazon: 'A terrifying story of a Nazi-inspired, bodged-up shark and its adventures – parts of the film seem a little far-fetched.'

What would have bumped up the value of my copy would have been if Clarke had inscribed a dedication to one of her children, too. And that would not be so unlikely since many of the poems in this slim fifty-four-page collection, the smallest book on the Welshly list, are about them.

As well as her children, Clarke's poems range over numerous other subjects – journeys, death, relationships, the natural world and colour – and their accessibility has made them popular inclusions on the A level and GCSE syllabuses. Two, in particular, stand out (and not just for me – J. M. Hindley, or perhaps another previous owner, has highlighted them on the contents page with light marks). In 'Catrin', Clarke remembers the birth of her daughter and how tightly bound they have been since her birth. Then, the dynamics of their relationship inevitably adjust as her baby becomes a teenager with her own separate identity and rebellious nature, yet she is still attached to her child. It ends with powerful lines, which all slightly worried parents will recognise, as Catrin asks if she can stay outside skating for another hour even though it's getting dark.

Ten pages later, Clarke presents the child–adult bond from a different angle. 'Baby-sitting' starts with the babysitter pondering her situation as she sits in an unfamiliar room, listening out for someone else's baby. The poem is all about the contrast between the connection with your own tiny offspring ('delightful, fragrant, can do no wrong') and the connection with somebody else's ('liable to unpleasant nose emissions, dodgy breath').

And it works both ways for the baby-sitter also feels sorry for the baby because when it wakes up, she's not going to like the stranger she finds watching over her one bit.

I also liked the title poem, 'The Sundial', about a child making a crude sundial with a stick and stones after suffering a sleepless and hot night of bad dreams, perhaps trying to control the sun's effect on him by marking its path.

Why this book matters... it paints a picture of Wales in a personal yet universal way.

Read it because... not enough people read good modern poetry.

Give it a miss if... you're just about to babysit.

What I discovered about Wales... Major Welsh poet Dewi Emrys (the subject of 'In Pisgah Graveyard' in the collection) paid a bar bill with a Bardic chair he won at the National Eisteddfod.

BOOK 27

SHOULD I STAY OR SHOULD I GO?

◆

On the Black Hill
by Bruce Chatwin
(1982)

Wales was a key location for that most intriguing of English writers, Bruce Chatwin. He spent time in and around the town of Rhayader and the Black Mountains area in Powys from childhood onwards, and his 1977 travelogue *In Patagonia* looks at the Welsh diaspora there. Even then, for a writer so closely associated with travel and nomadic lifestyles, it's perhaps rather unexpected that his first major piece of fiction should be a chronicle of twin brothers who barely set foot outside their rural Welsh farm during their entire lives.

On the Black Hill is a family saga that charts the long lives of Benjamin and Lewis Jones from their births (actually, from a bit before their births as the story includes how their parents met and courted) through the trials of their lives as farmers against the background of the First World War, up to the arrival of technology in the form of a video game in their local pub and their first tractor. While the action doesn't really move geographically, part of Chatwin's grand project with this novel is working through his more universal ideas on how to live the best life in a wider modern world.

Chatwin was at least partly inspired by a 1939 novel by German author Ernst Jünger called *On the Marble Cliffs*, which is a parable about Nazi rule and totalitarianism focused on two brothers whose lonely rural lives on cliffs close to the sea are endangered by malicious outsiders.

There's no real plot in *On the Black Hill*, just an episodic and fairly speedy, marking out of days (roughly a century is covered in just over 250 pages), with lots of little set pieces and a large supporting cast of local characters who pop up in little cameos. The twins represent the two sides of Chatwin's own personality and different approaches to restlessness. Lewis is the more archetypal heterosexual masculine male who does the heavy lifting around the farm, has 'a yearning for far-off places' and feels the stifling claustrophobia of home. Benjamin is asexual or possibly homosexual and does the cooking, and is more than delighted to stay at home. 'He never thought of abroad. He wanted to live with Lewis for ever and ever; to eat the same food; wear the same clothes; share a bed; and swing an axe in the same trajectory.' Despite their differences, they have a strong mystical connection that enables them to share physical peril when far apart.

In a 1970 magazine article for *Vogue*, Chatwin talked about one of seventeenth-century French philosopher Blaise Pascal's quotes from his book, *Pensées*: '*Tout le malheur des hommes vient d'une seule chose, qui est de ne savoir pas demeurer en repos, dans une chambre*' ('All unhappiness is down to one thing, man's inability to stay quietly in a room'). *On the Black Hill* is Chatwin's debate with himself about which is the right path to choose – contentment in a simple and settled home and the delights of the natural world or constantly searching for a nomadic nirvana. In the book there is a clear battle: town (essentially bad) versus country (essentially good, though by no means idyllic) or more concretely England versus Wales respectively (the brothers' cottage home and where they were born literally on the border between Wales and England).

The novel certainly rolls along at a heck of a pace and it has won plenty of plaudits, not least the Whitbread Best First Novel, a somewhat surprising victory given it was his second work of fiction. I did appreciate it, although it felt a little like a throwback to *The Battle to the Weak* in terms of its rural bleakness. It also felt a bit cold, a bit too observed and not genuinely emotional.

And I wasn't taken with Chatwin's, often, very staccato style. Here's an example when the brothers' English mother is on the receiving end of their less cosmopolitan Welsh father's anger:

> The crisis came when she experimented with a mild Indian curry. He took one mouthful and spat it out. 'I want none of your filthy Indian food,' he snarled, and smashed the serving dish on the floor. She did not pick up the bits. She ran upstairs and buried her face in the pillow. He did not join her. He did not, in the morning, make amends.

Aside from this, I found it thought-provoking and quite intense, especially the quandary that the twins' mother finds herself in – trapped in a loveless marriage in a 'gloomy house below the hill'. I would read it again.

This was another second-hand buy and, like *The Sundial*, also includes some remnants of the previous owner. Very detailed details, in fact, including not only their address (reasonably close to my home) but a phone number, too. I shall be discreet and not include them here but, Sally, if you fancy a reread, please do let me know.

Why this book matters... it shows how an older and a newer Wales connect on a human level.

Read it because... Chatwin blends fact and fiction like few other writers.

Give it a miss if... you like your drama seasoned with a little levity.

What I discovered about Wales... it was in many ways Chatwin's emotional centre.

BOOK 28

ONLY CONNECT

◆

Brothers
by Bernice Rubens
(1983)

More brothers. Lots more.

So far, most of the books on the list have included some look at the ins and outs of dual identities, but always on a Welsh-English axis, which is the main reason I included this on the Welshly list even though only about a fifth of the action takes place in Wales.

Brothers is another family saga, which stretches across six generations of a Jewish dynasty (even though it says four on the back-cover blurb). A family tree is helpfully included.

'Come, stranger, and hear the story of our constant flights from bondage and that of the minstrel who sings the song that orchestrates our survival,' it begins in ominous fashion. Rubens knows whereof she writes and regarded this as her finest work, although it was her other book, *The Elected Member*, that won the Booker Prize in 1970, making her the first woman to do so and the only Welsh winner to date. She was born in Cardiff to Jewish parents. Her father, Eli, was from Lithuania and her mother, Dorothy, from Poland. She uses her own family history and knowledge to tell the story of the Bindel family who are targeted by the Tsar's troops in 1830s Russia and then again in the 1871 Odessa pogrom. They emigrate to Germany and

Wales, endure the Nazi holocaust, return to Russia and finally head to Israel. Throughout, the Bindels' motto is 'only survive'.

On the positive side, *Brothers* is a remarkable educational tool. I suspect most readers will have some general knowledge about some of the events Rubens focuses on, like the Holocaust, but perhaps less about the earlier Russian pogroms. The book regularly sent me off to find out more details of exactly what happened, especially about the Jews who settled in Wales and numbered 5,000 at their peak around the end of the First World War. In this sense, it was an enlightening success.

As a novel, though, it works far less well. For a start, it crams in so much that there's no room for character development. People meet and get married within a couple of pages. The dialogue is clunky and wooden, and there's far too much exposition. When, on page 128, the Bindels head Wales-ward from Germany (Leon has a bit of trouble buying a ticket for the trip, 'there was something faintly unreliable about a country that even the ticket official had never heard of'), Rubens lobs this at the reader:

> The massive exodus from Eastern Europe began in earnest in the late seventies and continued until the passing of the Aliens Bill in 1894. During the first wave of trickling immigration, of which Aaron Bindel was a part, the Jewish Temporary Shelter was able to cater for all the needs of the improvident immigrant.

Yes, I immediately put the book aside to find out more about the Jewish Temporary Shelter, but it also brought any tension to a juddering halt.

Although only part of the action is set in Wales – where there is an obligatory mining disaster – the central themes of tradition and survival are as strongly to the fore here as elsewhere in the story. When one of the characters living in Cardiff decides to marry outside the Jewish community, he has to contend with his, to put it mildly, shocked family. This has an important bearing on the central issue of what survival means and what part assimilation plays in that. It does bear some comparison to the famous stage play and film, but it's a bit of a push to describe it as *Fiddler on the Roof* in Wales.

It's also unremittingly grim. Everybody – I mean *everybody* – has a terrible time and the plot moves from tragedy to tragedy across generation after generation. I realise that this is the central message: the ceaseless inhumanity shown to the Jewish community across Europe. But, by never letting up, it doesn't grip the reader, it only saddens and loses much of its emotional heft.

Once again, my 1988 Abacus paperback copy came from a local second-hand bookshop and once again, by chance, it contained something from a previous owner. In this case it was several lined notecards that contained addresses of people with Jewish surnames in Hendon, Stanmore and the city of Hod HaSharon in Israel. You don't get that kind of emotional postscript reading on an e-reader.

Why this book matters... it puts a part of the Welsh story in an international perspective.

Read it because... it's an important history lesson.

Give it a miss if... you're not good navigating complex family trees.

What I discovered about Wales... the history of Jewish immigration to the country.

INTERMISSION
Time for an ice cream

At this point, I am starting to get Welsh fatigue. This must happen to everybody with a similarly intense and challenging reading project. Even if you are loving your year-long dive into the complete works of Dorothy Whipple or Anthony Trollope, there always comes a point when you think that it's time for a palate cleanser and therefore reach for a Jilly Cooper.

And yet, it is not like I am wearily trudging through a big mandatory reading list and inwardly groaning about the seeming impossibility of getting through it. No, it's not like being a student at all. A major delight has been simply coming across authors whose names, six months earlier, had been as foreign to me as the latest online influencer. Rather than relying on a constant drip feed of the usual suspects ('Ah, I see William Boyd has a new one out.') or taking a lucky dip chance on the vast shelves of unreviewed books in my local bookshops, with the Welshly list I feel like I am ploughing new ground. While I usually avoid any opportunity to get out of my comfort zone, it does feel good sometimes to surge forward like a bookish panther into new places instead of shifting sideways like a literary crab.

Among the highlights so far has been wrestling (in a good way) with David Jones's *In Parenthesis*, which I actually took the opportunity to reread as per T. S. Eliot's personal instructions. And I *did* get more out of it a second time around, as he said I would, but I can't honestly recommend the collection as a read for your next beach holiday or city mini-break. Also from the poetry rack, my discovery of Lynette Roberts was a highly pleasurable moment. The most surprising find so far has been *Travels with a Duchess*, which was written with a kind of freshness that made it feel really quite contemporary, even though it's coming up to its diamond anniversary celebrations. Why Menna Gallie's book isn't far better known is slightly shocking to me. However, if I had to pick my *Desert Island Discs* book from the list at this stage, it would be Jeremy Brooks's *Jampot Smith*. While it's not groundbreaking in any literary sense – in fact, it's really quite straightforward – it captured the bittersweet experience of being a teenager in that way you occasionally come across when it feels like the author is writing specifically for you. There are several scenes that I can still picture in my head long after turning the final page.

Nevertheless, to be honest, Rubens's *Brothers* did feel like a good time to have a break and regroup for the coming assault on the summit. So I turned to my usual TBR pile, which was now really starting to put on weight after six months of my new Welsh diet, and got stuck into: *Tudor Children* by Nicolas Orme; *Sea of Tranquility* by Emily St John Mandel; *Demon Copperhead* by Barbara Kingsolver; *Winters in the World: A Journey through the Anglo-Saxon Year* by Eleanor Parker; *Flashman's Lady* by George MacDonald Fraser and *Yellowface* by R. F. Kuang. As none of these books are relevant to the Welshly quest in any significant way, I won't go into detail about them other than to say they were all absorbing but some of you will find Flashman's adventures offensive, so be warned.

At the same time, we had a family holiday to Wales. The five of us stayed in Y Felinheli next to the Menai Strait and had a great time. We went up Yr Wyddfa, visited the pier and my parents' former student digs in Bangor, mooched around Anglesey (although failed to see a single red squirrel. Boo.), enjoyed Caernarfon Castle, did a bit of kayaking, went to the cinema in Llandudno, and generally had a tremendous time. Everybody was delightful to us, especially a complete stranger in the local fish and chip shop who gave us some insider tips about where to get the best pies in the area.

I'm not unfamiliar with this part of Wales, but the experience of spending the previous six months reading virtually nothing else except books with some kind of Welsh theme gave the trip a quite different feel. For a start, I was much more aware of the Welsh language being spoken around me. I don't think on previous visits I had ever consciously noticed this. Perhaps it's due to the very welcome, growing number of Welsh-speakers, but it's certainly also because I now feel more attuned to the country and its culture and more interested in what is going on having packed some background knowledge along with my blood pressure pills into my suitcase. Connected to this is a greater appreciation for Welsh sensibilities, such as calling the mountain I'd always referred to as Snowdon by its Welsh name. Indeed, I looked at the whole Eryri region in quite a different light, having read the travelogues. Crossing the border from England to Wales and back again resonated more fully because of Raymond Williams's fine novel. I'm not suggesting, by any means, that in a week of being a tourist with my family, I'd miraculously developed a complete and meaningful knowledge of Wales, but it did all feel a little more familiar – a little more in focus. I even googled accommodation on Bardsey Island in an idle moment while waiting for my offspring to come down for dinner.

Perhaps most importantly, the upshot of that week in Wales is that I am feeling quite energised to hit the books again.

BOOK 29

GRUMPY OLD MEN

◆

The Old Devils
by Kingsley Amis
(1986)

Tastes don't half vary, eh? *The Old Devils* won the Booker Prize in 1986, beating off some fine competition that included Margaret Atwood's *The Handmaid's Tale* and featured fellow Welshly author Bernice Rubens as one of the judges. Kingsley's son, Martin, believed it to be his father's finest work, one that 'stands comparison with any English novel of the century'. *The New York Times* said: '*The Old Devils* is also Mr. Amis's most inclusive novel, encompassing kinds of feeling and tone that move from sardonic gloom to lyric tenderness.' What were they all thinking? They're wrong. All of them. It's terrible.

In *The Old* Devils, Alun, a minor-ish literary celebrity, returns to his previous home in Wales and his 'friends' who have never left there. They all drink an unbelievable amount of alcohol. Alun, although happily married, has casual sex with some of their wives, who, for no apparent reason, find him irresistible. The friends are all slightly unpleasant to each other. They moan a lot. One of them dies, but nobody really cares. Including me. Perhaps that was the point? Perhaps the joke's on me?

The Old Devils felt as distant, culturally, as *The Battle to the*

Weak, which was written a hundred years ago, and significantly more boring. Amis assembles a line-up of Roald Dahl grotesques who feel interchangeable other than their single defining characteristics: so there's a fat one, a dull one, one that's scared of the dark and one that is a full-blown alcoholic. The wives are even less distinguishable from each other. Other than to shake some general misogyny, Amis obviously couldn't be bothered to spend time on them.

Via his male mouthpieces, Amis also takes mirthless potshots at all kinds of typical Grumpy Old Men targets: modern music, modern pubs, modern young people, etc. 'I was laughing so much that I was frequently unable to continue reading,' commented *The Guardian*'s reviewer. Really? Did we read the same book? Substitute 'annoyed' for 'laughing' and that's how I felt well before I scrambled over the final page.

There's a thread running through the book about Welshness and fake Welshness, which is completely undeveloped. Alun is a thinly disguised Dylan Thomas figure (he is a fully paid-up disciple of the great man) who comes in for a lot of criticism for contributing to an overly romanticised view of Wales. It's never explained exactly why, but if you only have time to read either this or *Under Milk Wood*, there's absolutely no doubt which you should select. There are occasional flickers of interest in the theme of old age, but they're never developed either. It's not even as if the dialogue is any better. It's rambling, almost to the point of incoherence. I've read a couple of reviews of it comparing the narrative technique to some of Virginia Woolf's novels. It's true that there's some similarity but, frankly, I'd recommend *Mrs Dalloway* over this every time. The difference between them is the same as the difference between a thoroughbred horse and a donkey at the beach at Blackpool.

Even trying to be as even-handed as possible, the praise heaped on this book still seems simply misplaced. Amis's *Lucky Jim*, which owed at least something to his time working at Swansea University, is a classic. *The Old Devils* isn't.

Why this book matters... anything that wins the Booker probably can't be all bad.

Read it because... even if you don't like what he's saying, Amis writes very readably.

Give it a miss if... you're trying to cut down on your weekly units.

What I discovered about Wales... parts of it appear to be powered by whisky.

BOOK 30

A KIND
OF LOVING

◆

Work, Sex and Rugby
by Lewis Davies
(1993)

A friend of mine likes to play a lighthearted game that requires the literary competitors to sum up a book in two words. For *Work, Sex and Rugby*, I'd offer 'gently gritty'. The novel's publisher, Parthian, offer a slightly more elongated description: 'A Welsh homage to *Saturday Night, Sunday Morning*', which is much more helpful than my feeble effort.

Over four days and through 174 pages, we follow working-class Lewis, a young man whose bittersweet daily life is a routine of exactly what the title suggests. Between Thursday and Saturday, he works as a labourer on a building site with a philosophically gloomy boss, then he downs a drink or two in the local pubs (where he also downs a love rival in a bar brawl), conducts a one-night stand, and plays a bit of rugby. Rugby is, to be honest, why I picked this book because not to include at least some mention of the sport in a book about the literature of Wales felt disrespectful.

Although Lewis's existence is perhaps the kind of thing you might have winced at back in the day in *Loaded* magazine, he is rather unenthusiastic about everything he does in his dreary home town. He's stuck in a nihilistic rut without any real direction in life, especially when compared to his ex-girlfriend who is moving away in search of better things. Even the trinity of activities of the title provide him with little consolation. Lewis is more of a listless young man rather than an angry one. I found him quite likeable, though, and he reminded me somewhat of the character that Carmarthanshire-born actor Hywel Bennett played in the eponymous 1980s television comedy series *Shelley*. The author is also an enthusiastic supporter of Ron Berry's *So Long, Hector Bebb*, and so I felt there was some kinship between these two tragic protagonists.

There's lots of excellent writing here, including an especially marvellous description of being very drunk on a stag night at an Indian restaurant: 'Lewis rose unsteadily to his feet. He was not sure which direction to move but followed another customer who appeared to know where he was going.' When Lewis then gets slightly lost and ends up in a storeroom, sitting on some boxes for twenty minutes, I felt very seen.

Strangely, there's a startling final chapter in which Lewis morphs into the first-person narrator for a couple of pages – the literary equivalent of breaking the fourth wall in television or film. 'It's all a bit of a gimmick really,' says narrator Lewis, who then disappears again for the last few pages. It's certainly a bit odd, though the author's choice to call his main character by his own name (something that American novelist Paul Auster has made a habit of) means that, throughout the book, there are questions of exactly *who* Lewis is and how autobiographical we should understand the story to be. I'm not against playing with narration – I like Joshua Ferris's ingenious first-person plural narration in his *Then We Came to the End* and the double narrative switching between Esther and the more conventional omniscient narrator made no difference to my enjoyment of Charles Dickens's *Bleak House*. I just don't think it worked for Lewis – either of them – in this case.

Another oddity is the epigram at the start of the book – 'Who knows or dares to dream' – which is attributed to Simon Day. I can't find the source. Maybe it's the Simon Day from *The Fast Show*. The only other reference I can think of is the scene in the 1986 episode of *Blackadder II* (not written by Day) when Percy tries to create gold and ends up with a substance which Blackadder sardonically names 'green'. Can this really be what Lewis is referencing?

Lewis, the author, is certainly a lot more proactive than Lewis the builder's assistant. He set up the Parthian publishing house in Cardigan specifically to put out *Work, Sex and Rugby* and, following the book's success, developed it into a highly regarded independent publisher that supports Welsh authors writing in English.

My copy (a 1993 first edition) was again picked up in a second-hand bookshop and has, again, been signed by the author. A nice neat signature with an elongated upstroke on the L and an unexpectedly long downstroke on the D making it look like his name is actually Pavies.

Why this book matters... it acknowledges the importance of rugby to Welsh communities in a matter-of-fact way without any over-the-top purple prose.

Read it because... the curry night episode really is cringingly accurate.

Give it a miss if... you think young people should pull themselves together and just get on with it.

What I discovered about Wales... not everybody is having a great time living there.

BOOK 31

OFF TO A GREAT START

◆

Eucalyptus
Detholiad o Gerddi
(Selected Poems)
1978–1994
by Menna Elfyn
(1995)
◆

Translated by Gillian Clarke, R. S. Thomas,
Joseph Clancy, Nigel Jenkins, Elin ap Hywel,
John Barnie and Tony Conran

First, a confession. This book was also intended to include my account of learning Welsh from scratch in twelve months. I started off with the best of intentions and the constant upbeat encouragement of Duolingo, but by the time I reached this book – a bilingual collection of forty-five poems with the Welsh original and the English translation on facing pages – I realised that even my original goal of being able to read a fairly simple children's story in Welsh was grossly over-optimistic. That's not to say I didn't enjoy the temporarily halted journey of language learning, starting with classic Duolingo practice sentences such as 'Good afternoon, dragon and Emlyn' and moving on to master 'Owen is buying parsnips in Africa today' and the perhaps overly familiar 'Are you an unemployed actor?'

My level of Welsh fluency, at the point of opening *Eucalyptus*, was certainly nowhere near being able to grasp the magic of Elfyn's original Welsh text though, so I had to put my faith in the translators and despite their evident proficiency I always have a slight worry about that. The nineteenth-century English writer and traveller George Borrow, author of an 1862 travelogue *Wild Wales*, was a polyglot who learned the difficult Basque tongue Euskara and the Romany language into which he translated the 'Gospel of Luke'. He suggested that, rather than it being the 'other side of the tapestry' that Cervantes perceived, 'Translation is at best an echo'.

Even though Elfyn has said that 'I think all poets, in the end, would like to write poems that can't be translated,' she happily chose some excellent translators in R. S. Thomas and Gillian Clarke to enable me to enjoy her work. There are certainly some superb poems here, ranging widely from very personal pieces about miscarriage and the Welsh language to works that cover more general topics such as war and pacifism. Often, though they are generally short, one-page poems, they develop in unpredictable ways. For example, 'Strong Mints' – as short and perfect as an early Smiths song – begins:

> A sweet for Sunday
> where the tongue's dumb,
> a sermon to come

The piece then pivots to the final stanza:

> Mints of the burning taste
> of Welshness, strong
> on the scalded tongue.

And here's my favourite poem, 'Power Cut', which starts:

> A bit oftener than a blue moon
> it'll happen – night falls without warning
> We become gropers, feet feeling for paths

This poem then goes on delightfully about the surprising joys of having your electricity supply cut out before the inevitable moment when:

> Just as we were most enjoying it
> and the world stood still, electricity hit us
> stared like an accuser at our light-making
> and the gloom we'd cleverly made friends with.

More, I think, than any other poet I've read on the Welshly voyage, I've found that Elfyn is very good at starting a poem. She has a talent for gripping the reader immediately and making them want to read on, which is a skill as important in poetry as it is in prose. This is, after all, one of the ways you choose whether to buy a book or not while you're flicking through it in a bookshop. And as Woody Allen admits at the start of his film *Manhattan*, writers want to sell books.

One example of a skilful start from Elfyn is 'The Sunday Look of Swans':

> I'm suspicious of swan-lovers,
> those who linger beside
> the margins of a lake
> offering breadcrumbs
> biscuits and crisps.

And another is her poem 'First Sight of the Sea':

Our first sight of the sea
is the nearest we ever get
to discovering a marvel.

I tend to read poems a bit too quickly, but these are the kind of openings that encourage me to slow things down and properly relish them when I'm in something of a lazy reading mode.

Lazy is certainly not an accusation you could fairly level at Elfyn. In the introduction to this book, poet and translator Tony Conran described her as 'the first Welsh poet in fifteen hundred years to make a serious attempt to have her work known outside of Wales'. This might seem like a bit of a stretch but, as well as more than a dozen collections of poetry (translated not just into English but more than twenty other tongues, not to mention being the first Welsh language poet to be included in Transport for London's Poems on the Underground project), she has produced plays, libretti, non-fiction and novels for children. She has also been a national newspaper columnist as well as Professor Emeritus of Poetry at the University of Wales Trinity Saint David and President of Wales PEN Cymru. A passionate campaigner for the importance of the Welsh language and for nuclear disarmament, she's been imprisoned twice and arrested once for non-violent offences as part of acts of civil disobedience for both those causes. She's sat around daydreaming about sandwiches a lot less than me, for sure.

Again, this was a signed copy, which I bought second-hand. In fact, it was also inscribed by the author but I will spare the recipient's blushes...

Why this book matters... the dual language printing is not only useful but also a welcome alternative to learning how to say Egypt is not near Germany on a widely used language learning app.

Read it because... the takes on aspects of everyday life are spot on.

Give it a miss if... you're a swan-lover.

What I discovered about Wales... the delicious 'blwyddyn genedlaethol i'r ystlum' translates as 'national year of the bat'.

BOOK 32

BOOKS IN
THE RUNNING BROOKS

◆

Tree of Crows
by Lewis Davies
(1996)

Anti-pastoral writing has been with us almost as long as the
blissful, shepherd-friendly worlds that pastoral poets like
Theocritus and Virgil created. Here's the Duke in Shakespeare's
As You Like It. Banished from the court, he intends to make the
best of his new life and tells his loyal banished courtiers how
much he likes living rough in the forest.

> Now, my co-mates and brothers in exile,
> Hath not old custom made this life more sweet
> Than that of painted pomp? Are not these woods
> More free from peril than the envious court?
> Here feel we but the penalty of Adam,
> The seasons' difference, as the icy fang
> And churlish chiding of the winter's wind,
> Which, when it bites and blows upon my body,
> Even till I shrink with cold, I smile and say
> 'This is no flattery: these are counsellors
> That feelingly persuade me what I am.'
> Sweet are the uses of adversity,

Which, like the toad, ugly and venomous,
Wears yet a precious jewel in his head;
And this our life exempt from public haunt
Finds tongues in trees, books in the running brooks,
Sermons in stones and good in everything.
I would not change it.

But he does change it, and at the earliest opportunity. Although he's had a marvellous time under the greenwood tree, as soon as he can get back to the painted pomp of the envious court, he hurries home. More recently, while Thomas Hardy's works sometimes revel in the magic of the rural landscape, they also reveal it to be capriciously cruel and life-sapping. Welsh writer, critic and double (count 'em) Welshly-lister Raymond Williams has also poured scorn on the idea that urban life has destroyed a natural rural golden age as 'myth functioning as a memory'. Niall Griffiths's *Grits* – which is hurtling towards us on the near horizon – shows that the anti-pastoral is a theme present in modern Welsh writing in English, too. And Lewis Davies's *Tree of Crows* can certainly be described as anti-pastoral, but it can also be described as grim. The cast of *Hamlet* has a better survival rate. If you're looking for a novella that emphasises the realistic hardships of rural life and where shepherds have a hell of a time then you've come to the right place.

I picked this book after thoroughly enjoying Lewis's other novel, *Work, Sex and Rugby* – a book which has its sombre moments – but this next one is far more fatalistic. Set in a kind of Orwellian near-future, Nye and his brother Cain are sheep farmers in the bleak Welsh mountains. Their flock is being attacked, maybe by marauding wolves, but maybe by something else. Meanwhile, Nye's friend, Elan, is missing – it's presumed she has absconded with a group of local travellers who had been looking for crystals in the local quarry – and has not been seen for two years. Over a hundred intense pages, these narrative threads are resolved for good or bad (ok, for bad. It's all for bad. Right up to the last snap of a neck on the final page) in a sparse narrative style that feels like a crossover between Alan Garner's *The Owl Service* and his more recent *Boneland*.

A word on the book's title: the enigmatic first paragraph has a first-person narrator who is walking towards a desolate tree full to bursting with an apposite murder of crows. The birds fly away down the valley as the narrator approaches and muses: 'When I reach the end of the valley I know there will be no tree of crows.' The image doesn't reappear in the text. What does he mean? To be honest, I'm a bit stumped.

My 1996 copy has an interesting cover illustration that includes a piece of art by Gillian Griffiths of a bare tree in the foreground that looks like it is being blown in the wind. There is, what looks like, a huge mountain in the background, though it could possibly also be a dark thundercloud. Is this cover design, the book title and that first paragraph a reference to Caspar David Friedrich's 1822 painting *The Tree of Crows*? Friedrich was a master of the sublime landscape and the emotional reaction to nature. His *Tree of Crows* features a battered, leafless oak with a hill behind it and a number of crows hovering and perching within the branches. The oak and the crows are arguably a representation of death, while the brightening sky hints at a more optimistic future of salvation. So perhaps the novel's disquieting ending is not quite as gloomy as it may appear. Is it really about transcendence? I'd like to hope so.

Why this book matters... it's an impressive study of obsession.

Read it because... it maintains a chilly atmosphere in a granite-like, pared-back style.

Give it a miss if... you're considering becoming a farmer.

What I discovered about Wales... there's plenty more miles in agricultural markets yet.

BOOK 33

WHEAT IS THE HEAD OF THE TRAIN?

◆

Travels in an Old Tongue: Touring the World Speaking Welsh
by Pamela Petro
(1997)

There's a moment in this book that will resonate strongly with all authors. And not in a good way. 'Pardon me for being blunt,' says a redhead called Carol to Pamela Petro in the Churchill Bar of the British Club of Bangkok, 'but does your publisher really think there's a market for this book?' The answer is a resounding yes because this book is built around a wonderful concept.

Rather than a run-of-the-mill account of falling in love with Wales on a visit and gradually learning the lingo with hilarious misunderstandings along the way, Petro's book is a kind of inverted travelogue. Refreshingly, she makes absolutely no effort to buy a tumbledown farmhouse in deepest rural Wales where she can start shearing sheep. Instead, she spends half a year travelling around the world and visiting more than a dozen countries in Europe, Asia and South America – her visit to Patagonia at the end is a proper highlight – meeting up with groups of Welsh diaspora in each country. The motive behind her trip is to learn

Welsh. She argues that, in Wales, people are too ready to sidle into English when her not-entirely-perfect Welsh comes a bit of a cropper, meaning that she never gets enough practice and it's almost impossible to become fluent. These little pockets of Welsh speakers outside Cymru, she reasons, should provide a more immersive environment on the basis that, for example, a Spanish–Welsh bilingual is less likely to lapse into English. I'm not entirely convinced by her premise, but that's irrelevant because the story of her journey is genuinely fascinating and unlike any other travel book I've read before.

There is, as you might expect, a lot of exploration of the idea of what it means to be Welsh and whether there are degrees of Welshness. Petro ponders this regularly, especially when she encounters the Welsh folk in Thailand who speak no Welsh and appear to have no ongoing interest in the country of their origin, like Pat who, in a Bangkok bar, asks Petro, 'How can you feel such passion for Wales? We all couldn't wait to get out.'

We came across the Welsh word, *hiraeth* (a deep longing for home, specifically Wales) when we explored Raymond Williams's *Border Country*. Here we find its antithesis in a German word *fernweh*: a wanderlust that urges you to get the heck away from your homeland. The meeting in Thailand raises, in Petro's mind, the bizarre thought that perhaps she is the *most* Welsh of all those present. 'I've learned there exists a slippery sliding scale of Welshness,' she notes, though happily offers no definite answer to the question of how that is measured and leaves the reader to come to their own conclusions.

While I found this interesting, what I really identified with was her efforts to learn the language. The year *Travels in an Old Tongue* came out, I moved to Madrid with my wife where we lived for several years. At the point of expatriation, my Spanish was negligible and certainly not as good as Petro's Welsh, so I empathised with many of her worries and when she made linguistic mistakes. I'll never forgive the bartender who pretended he had no idea what beer I was ordering – a Mahou – instead of simply sighing, reflecting on the mangling of his native language by a gibbering no-nothing, and pouring me what I was *obviously* asking for. Pamela Petro certainly has the right idea about learning a language. Despite her awareness of her shortcomings and constant concerns about what Welsh speakers think of her proficiency in the language, she throws herself into it, which is, I think, the best way to do it. Some of this is purely physical. English writer George Borrow, whom we met in the last chapter, argued that his countrymen are the worst linguists in the world because 'when they attempt to speak Spanish, the most sonorous tongue in existence, they scarcely open their lips.' Petro is of a similar mind and works at getting her tongue and mouth around the sounds of her beloved adopted language. 'You can't just speak Welsh,' she says, 'you have to ride its waves.'

And ride the waves she does. Her linguistic adventures include failing to understand what's happening on the Welsh soap opera *Pobol y Cwm* (which I remember watching myself as a child in Shropshire in the early 1980s with ignorant fascination), a breakthrough moment when she's had a successful Welsh lesson, and the joy of being told she has no American accent in Welsh but more of a south Wales intonation with a Ceredigion lilt.

It's a very chatty, jolly read, and there are some very funny moments. At one point she is talking to a French railway conductor and only later realises he failed to understand her because she was mixing up French and Welsh and repeatedly asking him in rising panic, 'Wheat is the head of the train?' (*lle* [place] in Welsh sounds very much like *blé* [wheat] in French).

Although the book is mostly light in tone, there are serious moments. A discussion about bringing up children multilingually is a practical issue I have faced in my own English–Spanish–German domestic setup. But Petro is always honest about her unusual odyssey and ready to acknowledge the strangeness of 'an American trying to talk to a Swede in Welsh on the outskirts of Oslo'.

In the end, *Travels in an Old Tongue* is not a forensic investigation into the importance of learning another language. Even though the action takes place almost entirely abroad, Petro's endearing and infectious gusto for the language ends up providing a unique view of Wales, the Welsh language and the Welsh people through the eyes of people who no longer call it home.

Why this book matters... it shows that there's no shame in making mistakes while learning a new language.

Read it because... if you're learning a language it will inspire you to keep going.

Give it a miss if... you were hoping for another travel memoir about sheep farming.

What I discovered about Wales... 'llan' not only means 'church' but can also indicate something like 'sacred enclosure'.

BOOK 34

CARDIFF CALLING

◆

Five Pubs, Two Bars and a Nightclub
by John Williams
(1999)

Book titles matter. I'm not sure the world would hold such a
devotion for *The Great Gatsby* had F. Scott Fitzgerald stuck to
the title he really wanted, *Trimalchio in West Egg*. And Ernest
Hemingway made a wise choice when he swapped *I have
committed Fornication but that was <u>In Another Country and
Besides</u> the wench is dead* (the underlining was the author's own)
for, the rather more memorable, *A Farewell to Arms*. And I'm not
at all sure that *Five Pubs, Two Bars and a Nightclub* does justice
to what is a really engaging collection of short stories based in
the criminal underbelly of Cardiff's Butetown. I'm assuming
it's an ironic joke about *Four Weddings and a Funeral*, since the
subject matter could hardly be more different from the Richard
Curtis rom-com. The next two novels that follow this book in
Williams's city trilogy are *Cardiff Dead* and *The Prince of Wales*,
which strike me as much more buyer-friendly.

This book wears its cleverness very lightly. When it came
out, Williams was pigeon-holed with writers such as Irvine
Welsh, rather a lazy comparison since they don't feel akin at

all, other than not being set in the Home Counties. While it's not an unreasonable comparison, this group of interconnected short stories feels more like it's somewhere between Quentin Tarantino's *Pulp Fiction* and P. G. Wodehouse's *The Inimitable Jeeves*. It weaves what are essentially individual stories together into a quilt which, if not entirely seamless, is smartly brought together. I realise that this sounds like an unlikely literary cocktail, but there's an unforced humour in the stories that often reminded me of a rather turbocharged Bertie Wooster as I was reading. 'It was twenty years ago now,' says Ozzie, who is about to embark on setting up a pirate radio station in the city, 'but there was still a thrill attached to passing under a bridge you'd personally once blown up.' Think Arthur Daley with a dash of Guy Ritchie rather than Welsh's Renton and Begbie.

The novel is set in the multicultural Tiger Bay docks area just before it was utterly transformed by redevelopment. The book's title refers to the eight main settings for each story, which tie together in a kind of circular story arc. The first story opens with local gangster Kenny Ibadulla turning (not entirely successfully) part of his nightclub into a Nation of Islam mosque, and the final story features him fighting a turf war with another local hoodlum. In between, we meet sex worker Maria and her female pimp Bobby who get involved in a drug deal; a BBC television reporter who fakes a drug deal story (in which he laughs at the idea of the public being worried about local 'yardies' since 'the closest they've been to Jamaica's a day trip down Porthcawl'); and Tony who is recently released from prison makes a bid to escape a life of crime in Cardiff in the very filmic final chapter 'The Casablanca'.

On paper, this is the kind of disillusioned urban noir that I normally don't have on my bedside to-be-read list, but Williams creates an endearing dramatis personae of slightly desperate people living around society's margins that evokes the style of early twentieth-century New York short-story writer

Damon Runyon (*Guys and Dolls*) who specialised in colourful, picaresque tales about the underworld of gangsters and hustlers. Yes, it is seedy, but it feels very real and the characters are lively, charming and, above all, human. The situations are handled very winningly, too. The threat of violence – and sometimes more than the threat – hangs over the stories throughout, but so does a strong sense of humour. It's all done at an energetic and dramatic pace, too.

One of the reasons it's so good is that Williams knows the area well. Not only was he born and raised in Cardiff, but his previous book was *Bloody Valentine*, a true crime book about a botched murder investigation and miscarriage of justice in the city in the late 1980s. The people he met while researching the book inspired him to write *Five Pubs, Two Bars and a Nightclub*. The book of short stories so spoke to his hometown that he was delighted to discover via a bookseller that it was, by some distance, the most shoplifted book on their shelves.

Why this book matters... it offers a quite different perspective on daily Welsh life.

Read it because... it is much funnier than you might expect.

Give it a miss if... you're easily shocked.

What I discovered about Wales... it's surprisingly tricky to keep a pirate radio station up and running.

BOOK 35
THINGS FALL APART

◆

Grits
by Niall Griffiths
(2000)

All books play with language, but some frolic more than others. The first time I came across something that was not written 'properly' was Russell Hoban's post-apocalyptic *Riddley Walker* in my mid-teens, and I remember my first instinct was to bin it as I found it unreadable. This gave way, quite quickly, into delight as I realised I was able to 'translate' it. Since then, I've enjoyed the similarly post-1066 Battle of Hastings, textually-cryptic *The Wake* by Paul Kingsnorth (written in a form of recreated and modernised Old English), failed to get any kind of a hold on James Joyce's *Finnegan's Wake* ('experimental') and loved Mark Dunn's lipogram novel *Ella Minnow Pea* (written with progressively disappearing letters).

So I was certainly prepared to give Niall Griffiths's *Grits* – written in English, Welsh, and various phonetically transcribed regional vernaculars – a fair crack of the whip. Like *Riddley Walker*, Griffiths's characters exist in a world where things have gone very badly wrong for them, which has led each one to end up in a small town on the coast of Wales. So it doesn't feel like a barmy idea to let them tell their own story in their own language rather than the standard English you might find in a novel about a middle-class author's existential marriage crisis in his summer holiday home on the coast during a weekend with his siblings.

The action, such as there is, is semi-autobiographical and set in and around late-1990s Aberystwyth, which is Griffiths's adopted home territory. Alternating chapters are narrated in a kind of stream of consciousness by individuals from the group of heavy drug-using drifters – some Welsh but with many from elsewhere – often covering the same events but from different perspectives. We've certainly come a long way from *How Green Was My Valley* (though the character name Ianto features in both books. Griffiths's version reappears with a leading role in the follow-up novel, *Sheepshagger*) and are very much into *Trainspotting* territory here, constantly pungent language and all.

The linguistic barrier is very real and occasionally impenetrable, but overall not as inscrutable as Joyce's and, though I'm far from an expert, it did feel authentic. But I found it did slow me down so that finishing my 482-page 2001 paperback edition did turn into a bit of a long haul.

More of a problem than the linguistic styling was that it just didn't work for me – which is perhaps exactly what Griffiths intends since I doubt very much if I am his target reader. The episodic but plotless action with seemingly endless drug use and abuse just dragged on. The characters – united in a feral hatred of students – all felt too similar. Though there is considerable camaraderie within the group, it also felt rather depressing. There are plenty of issues raised about nationalism, nature (the book could be tagged under 'psychogeography'), and life at the bottom of the social pyramid, but the language and style obscured rather than enlightened those things for me.

Having said all that, there were some touches I did enjoy. One of the characters, Colm, is reading Cormac McCarthy's book *Suttree*, which features a group of people who are similarly at odds with the world. 'Amazin fuckin werds, in Cormac McCarthy. So ther a was, readin Suttree, all warm an sheltered from the rain. Oner the best nights av ad in fuckin ages. No craving, no hunger, no need, just safe an warm an comfortable.' Nice.

Why this book matters... it offers the chance to experience an underrepresented marginal voice.

Read it because... it's probably very unlike the rest of your TBR pile – and variety is the spice of life.

Give it a miss if... you don't like books that experiment with language.

What I discovered about Wales... the landscape provides inspiration to writers in quite different ways.

BOOK 36

A SMALL FIRE

◆

The Hiding Place
by Trezza Azzopardi
(2000)

When I think of horror fiction, it tends to be of the marauding zombies genre or demented killer type of thing. But on the basis that horror can be disturbing and, in fact, entirely realistic without bloody dismemberment, I think there's also an argument for placing this excellent though quite shocking novel by Trezza Azzopardi in the horror category, too.

The Hiding Place is the story of the Gauci family and begins with the arrival of Frankie to the Tiger Bay area of Cardiff in 1948 from Malta. Frankie marries Mary, who is Welsh, in the 1960s. The book concludes with a reunion of their children in the present day after the demolition of the Tiger Bay district has been pretty much completed. Frankie runs a café, but is a compulsive gambler and is involved with local gangsters within the Maltese immigrant community in which he and his family live.

Without descending into full misery melodrama territory, the youngest of his six daughters, the significantly named Dolores, narrates the family's traumatic trajectory as it spirals fairly hastily towards combustion. The family suffer poverty. Dol, as a newborn, suffers serious injuries and disfigurement – and consequent social stigma – in a house fire. One of her sisters is a pyromaniac, and another one exits the family unit in the kind of unexpected circumstance that caused me to put the book down for a minute and look at happy photos of my own children.

What's particularly effective is Azzopardi's understated approach to the subject matter she covers. It's unrelenting, but it's very matter-of-fact. Although Dol often gives her father a – very generous – benefit of the doubt, Frankie is an appallingly ruthless domestic abuser who is willing to do pretty much anything to make *his* life a little easier – this is a man who would literally sell his own children. But he's also a banal bogeyman, often a pitifully unlucky one, rather than an overdescribed monster from a horror film. Throughout, Dolores is an unsentimental narrator despite the trauma around her. She plays down her father's shortcomings while showing us that hiding places aren't always safe havens. Including for unfortunate pet rabbits...

The final section, set in the present day when gentrification has changed the city and area entirely, adds some different perspectives to Dol's story via her and her sisters' loving, if slightly brutal, reunion. It even casts some doubt on exactly how reliable a narrator she has been, and it becomes clear that this is also a novel about memory and how we (mis)remember early life ('a small fire is an inferno, a burnt hand is a horror story') as well as one about the importance of women sticking together against the threat from men. At the end, Dolores, who has become a librarian, is keen to make sense of her bleak early life ('I go back, and try to piece together how it was'), and this final part of the story shows her trying to put it all in order.

All in all, I found it an unsettling but completely gripping read, and the mix of fragmentary narrative techniques were stimulating rather than needlessly clever. The novel was shortlisted for the Booker but lost out to Margaret Atwood's *The Blind Assassin*. My only complaint really is that *The Hiding Place* ends on a huge 'What? Don't do that to me!' note that had me checking to see if there was a sequel. Sadly, it appears not.

Why this book matters… it adds an important layer to the immigration story of Wales.

Read it because… it's a proper page-turner.

Give it a miss if… you find it hard to read about children enduring abuse.

What I discovered about Wales… I hadn't appreciated how much redevelopment there has been in Cardiff.

BOOK 37

WHEN DRUIDS GO BAD

◆

Aberystwyth Mon Amour
by Malcolm Pryce
(2001)

We've already had a humorous novel on the Welshly list, but I'd like to put Amis's *The Old Devils* to one side for a moment (or even a lot longer) because this second entry is more than just a comic novel. It's also pastiche crime noir, set in a parallel universe Aberystwyth, written with deadpan humour – which is quite an ambitious amount to cram into 250 pages.

Humour is subjective. One person's barrel of laughs is another's lead balloon. I started off *Aberystwyth Mon Amour* with high hopes. I was looking forward to some jokes after an extended literary diet of – well – *no* jokes and people being very serious up mountains, on farms and in wars. And the premise seemed encouraging – an alternate present-day Aberystwyth that is run by a druid mafia in which a Sam Spade-like private detective called Louie Knight gets caught up in a mystery about disappearing schoolboys, which involves the legendary lost Welsh kingdom of Cantre'r Gwaelod. It's also the first of a series of six, so the public has clearly spoken about how much they like the books and the fantasy world he has created.

And Pryce certainly adds some inventive touches à la Terry Pratchett. He introduces the idea that Wales has fought its own Vietnam War in Patagonia, which is an interesting conceit. And I did laugh at the idea of a twenty-four-hour whelk stall and the delights of a glass of Ffestiniog Chardonnay (the seventy-three vintage is apparently really quite good). A friend who has read on through the rest of the series tells me that consulting detective Louie Knight moves his office in a later book to 221 Popty Street – *popty* being the Welsh word for bakery...

But it feels like Pryce is shoehorning too much into one package, and I was reminded of Douglas Adams's description of his own multi-sectional comic detective novel *Dirk Gently's Holistic Detective Agency* as a 'detective-ghost-horror-whodunnit-time travel-romantic-musical-comedy-epic'. There are scenes of much more than mild peril in Pryce's world – schoolboys are literally being murdered – but there's also the kind of 'wacky' sixth-form humour that names a central character who is very clever Dai Brainbocs. There's an attempt to add a hard-bitten edge to the prose, which is somewhere between homage and ironic send-up, but it's Raymond Chandler-ish and Dashiell Hammett-esque rather than the real thing. Don't come here looking for *The Thin Man*.

It all started to wear thin by the end for me in the same way that the literary high jinks of *The Eyre Affair* by Jasper Fforde – who took a similar comedy-drama route in his *Thursday Next* series – did. But it rattles along playfully, and if you think you will like Pryce's delight in world-building and think it's funny to call a philosophising ice cream barista Sospan, then you should dive right in.

Why this book matters... comic novels are ludicrously under-read, Welsh ones probably even more so.

Read it because... it's really unlike anything else on the Welshly list.

Give it a miss if... you find Terry Pratchett's humour too wacky.

What I discovered about Wales... Cantre'r Gwaelod (I spent ages going down an internet rabbit hole reading about it).

BOOK 38

MICHELANGELO IN BLAENAU FFESTINIOG

◆

Framed
by Frank Cottrell-Boyce
(2005)

To be honest, at this point, with three dozen books in my wake, I genuinely considered packing the Welshly list in. Three of the last four books had left me wondering if my book choice antennae had gone wonky or if the whole idea was too ambitious or, even less palatably, if I was turning into an even grumpier middle-aged man than I already was. And to be equally honest, after the *Chronicles of Prydain* non-starter, I was not wholly in the mood for another children's title.

So, naturally, this one turned out to be an absolute cracker. For me, it's one of those books you get so childishly excited about that you want to check with everybody you know whether they've read it and whether their children have read it. In fact, I'm a bit embarrassed I didn't lob it to my children when they were younger, as they would have loved it. In terms of characters, it has some fabulous nippers, plenty of easily bamboozled adults, and a plot that is interesting historically. I'm smiling just thinking about the book as I type this.

Framed takes inspiration from a true story. In late August 1939, the National Gallery in London took precautionary measures to avoid its artworks being destroyed during the bombing of the capital by moving most of its collection to Wales. For a couple of years, a remote and abandoned slate mine in the mountains of north Wales was housing two thousand pieces of art, including works by big hitters such as Rembrandt and Monet. Here, they were secured inside half a dozen underground brick storerooms fitted with air-conditioning systems. It was a sensible move. The National Gallery was bombed nine times during the Second World War.

In the present day, nine-year-old Dylan is the only boy, of football-playing age anyway, in the tiny Welsh village of Manod, where his parents run the not-very-busy Snowdonia Oasis Auto Marvel garage. One day, a convoy of lorries turns up in this sleepy part of the world and heads up the mountainside. Dylan's knowledge of the *Teenage Mutant Ninja Turtles* leads him unexpectedly into the world of artistic masterpieces and one thing leads to another and – well, let's just say you'll be surprised what happens to Van Gogh's 'Sunflowers'.

Dylan is a particularly endearing character. Manod is not the most exciting place in the world to grow up in. It's grey, damp, economically starved and haemorrhaging population, but Dylan looks largely on the bright side. Cottrell-Boyce does a convincing job of portraying him as bright but still not mature enough to quite understand what is happening around him, especially his father's worries about the garage's uncertain future. There are some excellent other residents of Dylan's world, including his sister, Marie, whose ambition is to become a criminal mastermind. His neighbours are two elderly sisters who work as a not wholly unsuccessful team to drive their single car: one can't see and one can't steer. Locals don't complain about the consequent likelihood of carnage; they simply time their own shopping trips into town accordingly.

Framed is funny throughout. At one point, the family's stock of breakfast cereal runs out, so Dylan decides to have a Mars bar instead.

> 'That is so unhealthy,' said Marie. 'You can kill yourselves if you like. I'm going to sort out a proper breakfast for myself.' She had a Bounty, because they've got real coconut in them, which is very good for you.

Without battering the message home, *Framed* is also about the importance of art in our lives. The paintings unexpectedly tiptoe into the villagers' lives and change them fundamentally, not because of their monetary value, but because they enrich life in Manod in so many other different ways. They literally brighten up their lives and deepen community spirit. Moronic politicians who scorn the value of the arts should be made to read this book out loud from the stocks.

Maybe it's a little bit too long at the 310 pages in my 2005 Macmillan edition, but it's also admirably cheery and positive. Hooray!

Why this book matters... it's a proper feel-good story but with an important and serious underlying message.

Read it because... it's tremendous fun.

Give it a miss if... I can't think of any reason to. Not a single one.

What I discovered about Wales... The A496 (which features heavily in the story) is high on the list of road accident blackspots in the UK.

BOOK 39

SMALL IS GOOD

◆

Fresh Apples
by Rachel Trezise
(2005)

As a teenager, I much preferred short pop songs such as Primal Scream's 'Velocity Girl' or The Smiths' 'This Charming Man' to the seemingly endless album version of Prince's 'Purple Rain' or the tracks on Dire Straits' album 'Love Over Gold' (five tracks in forty-one minutes? No thank you, sir). But while I turned my nose up at extended musical works, I have been more than happy to tuck into ludicrously long epic books such as Frank Herbert's *Dune* series or Stephen Donaldson's often baffling *The Chronicles of Thomas Covenant* series.

And yet, as I've got older, so the appeal of long novels has faded. Vikram Seth's 1,500-pager *A Suitable Boy* would certainly make my ten favourite reads list, but the truth is that I read it in 1994 when I was an all-powerful twenty-five-year-old, and thirty years later I baulk at anything even half that long. It's a shallow and philistine attitude, and I readily acknowledge it's me and not them.

So it probably won't knock you sideways when I reveal that these days, the Claire Keegans and the Muriel Sparks of this world have increasingly caught my eye in a literary version of the distracted boyfriend meme. But, while it would be unfair to say I liked *Fresh Apples* entirely because the eleven short stories in this collection only amount to a total of 170 pages, I will admit that, when the book arrived in the post, I was pleased to see it was small enough to fit through my narrow letterbox.

I may have given the impression during my summaries of the last few Welshly choices that I dislike unflinching modern novels that confront the everyday traumas we face in our modern age. The truth is that I simply find them a bit too unrelenting. I prefer my dose of stark reality with a little bit of leavening and, ideally, some badminton in the back garden to help me relax. This collection provides exactly that – minus the badminton. The stories are set largely in the economically challenged towns in her Rhondda Valley home and focus on the lives of teens and twenty-somethings, but the action also moves further afield to London and the USA. The vivid stories do not flinch from distressing situations – sextortion, suicidal ideation, international smuggling and stalking – which are mostly women suffering at the hands of men.

But the collection is not all unremittingly bleak. The stories are often very funny, although they tend to be towards the black comedy end of the spectrum. What Trezise does so well, as John Williams does in *Five Pubs, Two Bars and a Nightclub*, is understand that there is often light in even the darkest moments of life. Her story about a druggie holiday to Cornwall, *The Magician*, is in some ways as bleak as *Grits* but feels far less apocalyptic. For me, that not only feels like a more realistic take on life, but it makes me more likely to read the work. I'm not alone. *Fresh Apples* sold well, especially after Trezise won the inaugural Dylan Thomas Prize in 2006, and the chairman of the judging panel, scriptwriter Andrew Davies, compared it favourably to James Joyce's *Dubliners*.

All of the simply told and emotionally powerful stories in this collection have an element of humour, but they also often have unexpected final twists. One of the best is 'Chickens', in which

Chelle disastrously mishandles her grandfather's chickens in his Treorchy garden. Her growing realisation of what she's done and the appropriateness of her punishment is treated wittily rather than darkly and is cleverly interwoven with the reappearance of an important family member right at the end of the tale. The last story, 'The Brake Fluid at Gina's', set at a mechanic's garage in Pontypridd, is also elegantly done. A stalker briefly reappears in his girlfriend's life before getting a decisive comeuppance. These are not laugh-out-loud stories, and it's hard to feel too optimistic about the characters' futures after the curtain falls at the end of each one, but a video of me reading them aloud would have recorded plenty of wry smiles.

You will find that all uncomfortable bittersweet human life is here. And in 170 pages, too, mark you.

Why this book matters... it's a glittering kaleidoscopic look at Welsh youth today.

Read it because... the change of gears in the storytelling keeps you absorbed.

Give it a miss if... you've always thought that what 'Telegraph Road' by Dire Straits needed is an extended remix.

What I discovered about Wales... it's nice to know that the Mari Lwyd custom (a wassailing folk custom using a hobby horse made from the skull of a horse) is fondly thought about.

BOOK 40

A SEARCH FOR A STORY

◆

Running for the Hills:
A Family Story
by Horatio Clare
(2006)

Farming sometimes looks like it's a bit of a doddle, doesn't it? Ok, there must be various ups and downs, but just like we approach the dramatic peril injected by Kevin McCloud into *Grand Designs* with comfortable scepticism, we know it's all going to turn out nice again in the end, don't we? Judging by the various memoirs out there, everybody seems able to just turn their hand to becoming an olive oil producer or a lemon grower. Hey diddle de dee, a farmer's life for me! *Running for the Hills: A Family Story* offers us a taste of the fuzzier end of the lollipop.

   Although there are some of the usual suspects when it comes to a farming memoir here (no running water, rugged scenery, an ancient farmstead and unbelievably helpful neighbours), several things make it different from other 'sheep on the mountain' titles on the Welshly list. First of all, it's told mostly through Clare's own memories of his childhood rather than that of an ambitious young adult trying their hand at farming for the first time. As a result, we get an interesting partial picture of how life on this farm unfolded in the 1970s.

And then there's the way it unfolds. No spoilers, but if Thomas Firbank's *I Bought a Mountain* and Ruth Janette Ruck's *Place of Stones* made you quite fancy having a shot at getting up at silly o'clock to rid your own flock of livestock of wiggly things, then *Running for the Hills* will give you pause for thought. To put it politely, mistakes are made and the financial peril that is inherent on many farms is apparent on almost every page.

That said, it's not really about farming at all. A major strand of the story is the breakdown of the marriage of Clare's parents, Jenny and Robert. This happens for various reasons, but certainly among them is the constant battle of trying to make money from their farm. Jenny is compulsively committed to the project, which has taken them out of London and into 72 acres the other side of the Black Mountains. Robert is certainly up for having a go but is more realistic about the whole enterprise. Readers will have their own opinions about who makes the right decisions, both in terms of farming and parenting.

The first quarter of the book is written like a novel or a dramatisation with a third person narrator and is put together using conversations Clare had with each of his parents, their own diaries and, as Clare admits, his own imagination and dramatic licence. It's all very intimate and, though Clare says in the preface that he has tried to tell the story as truthfully as he can, sometimes I felt like I was intruding on the private life of the family. There's a lot going on in this book, which – whether you call it creative non-fiction, nature writing (there is plenty of this and it is atmospherically done) or memoir – is very definitely not a 'How to Farm' handbook.

Clare himself has called the book 'a search for the story of what [had] happened to my parents'. It is an impression of his own experience. He describes his childhood as 'beautiful and extraordinary' and one that he wanted to share as a testament to his mother. Although he is even-handed throughout in his consideration of his mother, he says: 'I believed in her philosophy

– live and let live, live now, live with the natural world.' I found *Running for the Hills* a less than optimistic and inspiring read, however honest and laudable the intentions, but I suspect other readers may find it passionate and mesmerising.

Why this book matters... it feels like an honest account of an uncommon childhood.

Read it because... the childhood view of relationships is fascinating.

Give it a miss if... you're going through a marital breakup (although it may perhaps also be helpful).

What I discovered about Wales... the first first farming book on the Welshly list was set almost a hundred years before this book, and it's still clearly a hard grind to make farming work commercially.

BOOK 41

ANOTHER MURDER
OF CROWS

◆

Martha, Jack & Shanco
by Caryl Lewis
(2007)

◆

Translated by Gwen Davies from the Welsh
Martha, Jac a Sianco (2004)

As the Welshly list has moved from the twentieth to the twenty-first century, the writing has certainly got darker. Caryl Lewis's story of three middle-aged siblings on the family farm in west Wales is certainly no exception. There are occasional lighter moments, but this book is, overall, a claustrophobic drama. One of the most memorable scenes – and one that sums up the feel of the book – for me is a couple of stomach-churning pages when two of the brothers are treating lambs who have maggot infestations.

We're in familial territory with Bruce Chatwin's *On the Black Hill* here. Although the siblings' parents are dead, the tentacles of their legacy linger on. Martha is the motherly rock of the group but is dealing with her own commitment issues in her relationship with her remarkably patient suitor, Gwynfor, because it would mean leaving the family farmhouse, Graig-ddu (Black Rock).

One of the many very human touches in the novel is the scene where Martha preserves the footprint Gwynfor left in the garden the day she turns down his marriage proposal using an upturned washing bowl. Jack is miserable, miserly and unwilling to move on from his father's traditional farming methods but is, nevertheless, unhappy with how the farm is running. And his brash new English girlfriend seems keen to make big changes, which feels like a comment on the changes a new century brought to traditional Welsh life, not least from English incomers from the east. Shanco has an unspecified learning disability and a more minor role in running the farm but ultimately has the biggest impact on the family unit. If that hasn't made it clear, there are not many laughs in these 185 pages. Bottom line: nobody is going anywhere and everybody is having a rotten time.

The writing and the characterisation are excellent, as you would expect from a title that won Welsh Book of the Year in 2005. Lewis is particularly good at exploring the relationships between the siblings but also the animals that surround them on the farm. Jack's understanding with his sheepdog, Roy, and Shanco's with his terrier, Bob, are very well observed. So is the unnerving presence of crows in the story.

It's at this point where I really do regret my lack of ability to cope with anything more complex in Welsh than 'Dewi is eating parsnips in the pub'. *Martha, Jack & Shanco* was originally published by Parthian in Welsh as *Martha, Jac a Sianco*, and two years later became available in an English translation by Gwen Davies. She has won universal praise for her work on it so it would be fascinating to compare the original to the translation. Davies has talked about the key interpretive role translators play in rendering one text into another. Here she is, for example, in an interview with *Wales Art Review*:

> My response to the challenge of translating the narrative-level dialect in *Martha* had been to

make the authorial voice more intimate (which dialect naturally conveys but which I didn't want to introduce into the main voice because of that class-place tangle). These were instinctive decisions rather than theoretical ones.

I give Davies full marks for a translation that doesn't feel in the least stilted, but my ongoing personal reservations are about a text that is quite so glum.

Why this book matters... it shows why reading in translation can be very rewarding.

Read it because... emotionally, it's beautifully observed.

Give it a miss if... you have a fractious relationship with your siblings that you don't want to be reminded about.

What I discovered about Wales... farming can be a love-hate career.

BOOK 42
PUSHY PARENTS

◆

Gifted
by Nikita Lalwani
(2007)

By chance, the next title on the list also features a writer making sense of real-life events through an imaginative prism, if that doesn't sound too pompous. While Horatio Clare 'recreated' conversations between his parents before he was born, Nikita Lalwani's story of Rumi Vasi, a schoolgirl and maths prodigy, is set in Cardiff – where Lalwani grew up with her Sindhi Hindu parents – but is inspired by the real-life experience of Sufiah Yusof. After a pretty strict home-schooling regime designed by her father, Sufiah started studying maths at Oxford at age thirteen. Her relationship with her parents, whom she said had pushed her too hard, imploded when she was fifteen and she was taken in by a foster family. The British media, eager to find a story demonising immigrant families, hounded and harassed Sufiah for years after that.

In *Gifted*, Rumi Vasi is recognised as a potential maths marvel at the very start of primary school. From the age of five, she is pushed hard by her first-generation immigrant father, Mahesh, a mathematics academic in Swansea, and her mother, Shreene. Under their academic and socially restrictive strict regime, she whizzes through her exams with her – or at least her parents'

– eyes firmly set on a place at Oxford, which she secures at age fifteen. Then the wheels come off.

There are several stories here, and they are told from multiple viewpoints, which gives the reader insights into the protagonists' thought processes, which they tragically fail to share with each other. So we are privy to Mahesh's ambition to prove himself in his adopted country and Shreene's growing dislike of English society. But *Gifted* is, at heart, a rites of passage novel about the dangers of hothousing and Rumi's struggle to then lead a normal teenage life. Superbly done, it deserved its place on the Booker longlist 2007 and the Costa First Novel Award shortlist. The will-they-won't-they relationship she has with one of the boys at her school feels wincingly authentic as they dance around each other's emotions. Her increasing social isolation and loneliness is also compellingly conveyed as the well-intentioned but, in truth, tyrannical parenting becomes excruciatingly difficult to witness. In the earlier sections of the book there's plenty of comic relief, but this gradually disappears as Rumi gets older and her life takes a darker turn, including a surprisingly horrific cumin seed addiction.

My major quibble with the book is about Rumi's maths ability. Lalwani is excellent at showing us that Rumi is, despite her father's indoctrination, more interested in boys and books than maths. She likes maths, she is very good at maths, but is she a maths genius? There are a few slight scenes when she talks about how she sees and feels about numbers and references to Venn diagrams, but while she's obviously bright she doesn't feel light years ahead of her school peers, and when she gets to Oxford she appears completely out of her depth academically from the very beginning. So why did the Oxford mathematics department make her an offer? It doesn't make sense

I also have a few minor quibbles about the Oxford section as I was there at exactly the same time as Rumi turns up and some of it just doesn't quite ring true to me, though people do have very different university academic experiences I suppose. It's also hard to believe that her parents rather leave her to her own devices at university having been breathing down her neck constantly over the previous decade. When another teenage prodigy Ruth Lawrence went to Oxford in the 1980s her father was regularly near her side, at lectures and cycling around town, wisely making sure she was ok.

Gifted is mostly set in Cardiff and is written by an author who grew up there, so it certainly isn't a rogue entry on the Welshly list but it does wear its Welshness very lightly. Where some other books, including understandably the travelogues, are often steeped in Welsh language and culture, by contrast, Lalwani concentrates more on evoking the 1980s (cue references to Rubik's cube and The Cure) and less on cartographic namedropping. The result is that it feels more like a book set in Wales than about Wales.

Why this book matters... it will hopefully help to deter damaging hothousing of talented children.

Read it because... it's not a bad depiction of what the general Oxford experience is like.

Give it a miss if... you find depictions of authoritarian parenting (however well-meaning) distressing.

What I discovered about Wales... its primary teachers appear to be remarkably proactive.

BOOK 43

WHAT IF?

◆

Resistance
by Owen Sheers
(2007)

One of the beauties of a reading programme is that you have no idea
where it's going to take you. I had not expected thirty-seven books
ago that my technical knowledge about lambing would have become
quite so extensive (yes, this is another 'sheep in the valley' book,
though it's also much more than that). Another is that, after a while,
you start to see through the glass less darkly as familiar elements
from previous reads reappear in current reads. Tyler Cowen, on the
Tim Ferris podcast, advised reading books in groups focused on the
same topic and then you can 'do a kind of cross-sectional mental
econometrics and see which pieces start fitting together'. And, at
this point in my own reading, I did start to feel that the Welshly list
was starting to form, dot-to-dot, a recognisable picture, and that
was despite the inevitable jeopardy of my scattergun approach to
pulling it together. And so I think I see what Tyler meant.

Novelist Anthony Powell – who claimed descent from the
twelfth-century ruler of south Wales Rhys ap Gruffydd and
published dozens of papers on Welsh genealogy, a subject he
described as illustrating 'the vast extent of human oddness' – puts
it very nicely in his novel *A Question of Upbringing*, the first in his
Dance to the Music of Time series. He describes the phenomenon
of how people appear and disappear in our lives seemingly without

meaning, but these meetings eventually serve a purpose 'in evolutions that take recognisable shape'. It's taken a while, but I'm starting to get shape vibes when it comes to Welsh writing.

As I read *Resistance* a novel by Welsh poet Owen Sheers, I began to see shades of books that had gone before in the Welshly list. David Jones appears again, last seen in *In Parenthesis* (Book 2). The story of the world-famous works of art hidden in rural Wales, which I joyfully encountered in *Framed* (Book 38), also makes a happy reappearance.

Resistance starts at an apocalyptic moment in an alternative world history, not as apocalyptic as Douglas Adams's *The Hitchhiker's Guide to the Galaxy* or Cormac McCarthy's *The Road*, but still pivotal. It is 1944 and Nazi Germany has successfully invaded England after the failure of the Normandy landings. In the remote Olchon valley in the Black Mountains, the wives in a tiny farming community wake up one cold winter morning to find that their husbands have silently disappeared during the night. Soon afterwards, a small band of handpicked German soldiers arrives on a seemingly peaceful but clearly important and undisclosed mission. Although this is a story about the effects of war on the abandoned wives, the soldiers and the local civilians, the main focus is on the relationship between Sarah Lewis and the Nazi commanding officer and intellectual, Albrecht Wolfram.

These 'what if?' takes on history, like Robert Harris's *Fatherland* and Philip Roth's *The Plot Against America*, depend very much on how realistic the alternative story comes across. Sheers was actually inspired by stories of civilian sleeper cells in Wales and elsewhere known as Auxiliary Units, which were established at the start of the war in case the worst happened. Naturally, though, he also has to make a lot up. One controversial decision he made was to set *Resistance* in 1944 following a failed D-Day rather than earlier in the war, say 1940, when Germany was much stronger. However, while it might upset some history scholars and meteorologists who argue that it was actually 1947 when Wales endured a terribly harsh winter, it's important to remember that this *is* an entirely different reality that Sheers has created. It is one where Churchill pushes off to Canada, and Roosevelt loses that year's US election. It's also important in terms of the plot that it is set later in the war when the German soldiers are largely sick of the whole endeavour rather than earlier on when they were more eager for the fray.

Sheers is a poet and tells the story at a lingering rather than punishing pace, more *Inspector Morse* than *Midsomer Murders*. There's also plenty of ambiguity in the novel – what exactly happens to the men who disappeared is never fully explained, although there are hints. Rather, this is the story of the women's resistance to invasion. It's certainly not the place to come if you're looking for big set-piece fight scenes – although there are a couple of unpleasant moments that are all the more powerful for being few and far between and treated with a lack of sensation.

There is also plenty of nature writing. The landscape and the women's and invading soldiers' reaction to it are central to the action. The valley is so cut off that its population believe it to be something of a safe haven until it gradually becomes more dangerous. For the invading German soldiers, it's almost the other way around as it becomes a refuge for them from the war. The sleeping army of volunteers that arise at a time of peril is a modern echo of the story Sarah fondly remembers the poet David Jones telling her in person where knights, led by King Arthur, awaken from their slumbers in a cave when they are most needed to defend their country. Or, as he puts the tale in *In Parenthesis*, 'his mess-mates sleeping like long-barrow sleepers, their dark arms at reach'. Indeed, Albrecht's name is presumably a nod to the thirteenth-century German knight and poet Wolfram von Eschenbach, who wrote *Parzival*, the early Arthurian Grail poem and tale of love and chivalry.

Resistance is a story about borders and how geography affects our everyday lives. The Olchon valley is not too far from the Welsh border with England. Sarah muses while browsing the names that come before her in the family Bible.

With each new wave-hill that rolled them nearer England, with each man that took them east, their names were smoothed in the wash of the tide. The *Mabinogion* was replaced by the Bible and the ornate Welsh was rounded and buffed to the simpler shapes of English.

And, without giving too much away, the remarkable piece of art that the German soldiers seek, which is at the heart of the plot of *Resistance*, is another medieval creation and has a strong whiff of anti-Semitism about it.

In 2016, a letter written by David Jones to Anthony Powell came up for auction at Bonhams. In it, he talked about the history of Wales and the lack of 'visual, tangible, concrete "remains" of the genuine Welsh past'. He wrote it on the anniversary of the First World War assault he chronicles in *In Parenthesis*, and 'What a long, long time ago that ... period now seems'. While the action of *Resistance* does not offer us any tangible remains, it does remind us that questions about how we deal with the vicissitudes of war and oppression are still very relevant to us in the twenty-first century.

Why this book matters. . . it's refreshing to read a story involving Nazis that isn't just all about the men.

Read it because. . . I bet you won't guess how it ends.

Give it a miss if. . . you think alternative history speculations are pointless.

What I discovered about Wales. . . the existence of the Auxiliary Units during the Second World War plus the extent to which remote valleys could be so disconnected from the nearest settlement.

BOOK 44

BRAVE NEW WALES

◆

Twenty Thousand Saints
by Fflur Dafydd
(2008)

Although I had some mixed feelings about Brenda Chamberlain's
Tide-race (Book 17), Bardsey continued to intrigue me and
to exert some kind of inexplicable pull. So, I thought a return
to Ynys Enlli with a more modern guide would provide some
twenty-first-century context. Moreover, Fflur Dafydd is the
daughter of poet Menna Elfyn, whose *Eucalyptus* (Book 31) I
liked so much that I reread it once I realised the connection and
enjoyed just as much the second time around.

Dafydd built *Twenty Thousand Saints* on her earlier work
written in Welsh, *Atyniad*. It will be interesting to compare the
two once I can get my own Welsh beyond 'Egypt is not near
Germany' on Duolingo, since the English version is apparently
significantly different in terms of plotting and characters.

An apposite Brenda Chamberlain quote from *Tide-race* starts
Dafydd's book: 'Life on this, as on every small island, is controlled
by the moods of the sea; its tides, its gifts, and its deprivations.' It's
as true this time round as it was then, that the characters' lives are
ruled by the whims of the water and the tides that seclude them

from the world beyond. Indeed, while I was writing this book, the BBC screened a three-part series called *Pilgrimage: The Road Through North Wales* in which various celebrities took a spiritual walking tour around the region. The finale was meant to cover a journey to Bardsey Island, but, on the day of the crossing, the sea was too rough, and they had to make do with a very windy view of it from the mainland. Not great television, frankly, but definitely a testament to the power of nature.

Like Pryce's *Aberystwyth Mon Amour*, *Twenty Thousand Saints* packs a lot in. The story is set against the backdrop of Welsh nationalism from the 1979 devolution referendum to the opening of the Welsh Senedd. It's an intense summer murder mystery that features several love stories, more than a splash of comedy and a touch of horror. Leri and Greta (one of whom has a hidden agenda) are television documentary filmmakers who head to Bardsey, where they find plenty of villagers who are understandably a bit suspicious of the temporary blow-ins as well as a rule-bending hermit, an archaeologist who has returned home to dig into the past and a visiting writer-in-residence. It's great, but the constant switching between storylines can be a little dizzying, especially once the action hots up about three-quarters of the way through.

Twenty Thousand Saints is a book about many things – but it is especially about change. Viv, a nun and slightly maverick hermit (who is hosting a conference of fellow hermits from around the country as the book opens, one of the funniest set pieces), goes through an examination of her nationalist leanings. Writer Mererid tries to resolve her doubts about her forthcoming marriage. Everybody thinks they know how Viv's friend, Delyth, disappeared suddenly from the island but they are forced to reassess their watertight convictions when her son Iestyn returns unexpectedly. At the centre of it all is the island itself – 'our own little Wales' according to the young utopian Viv – that offers them all space to explore their true feelings away from the lures of the mainland where people appear to live unfulfilled lives. Although mainland, Wales, too, is changing, as Viv finds out at the very end of the book.

Crucially, Dafydd's book is also about the Welsh language and what it means to speak it or decide not to speak it. The returning archaeologist is Viv's brother, Deian, who is digging into the past but has come to believe that Welsh is now a long-gone part of his youth as he has spent his adult years in Preston. He feels that he's lost 'the language of the island and his childhood... their own little enclosed world.' He tells the filmmaker, Greta, that it 'faded' and she's horrified.

> 'Why do people let that happen?' Greta let out. 'For someone just to lose a language like that... happens all the time with Welsh, it's like they think it isn't really important.'

He's also brought up short by the arrival of his close boyhood friend Iestyn, recently released from prison, who rubbishes Deian's logic.

> 'You are joking? How the fuck can you manage to lose your Welsh after a few years over the border and mine stays intact after ten years at Her Majesty's Service?'

In fact, Iestyn makes a rather telling point.

> 'They were all bloody speaking Welsh in Cardiff when I came out, I tell you. Like bloody geese they were about that castle. And I get here and I can't find one Welsh speaking fucker to talk to.'

Wales is changing, says Dafydd, and it's important to keep up.

Why this book matters... it gives the Bardsey story – and the story of Wales – a more up-to-date wash and brush up.

Read it because... how many other books about modern hermits have you read?

Give it a miss if... you think being a hermit is no laughing matter.

What I discovered about Wales... R. S. Thomas was the first chairman of the Bardsey Trust Council, established to preserve the island's spiritual and ecological heritage, and wrote a poem about it, *Pilgrimages*.

BOOK 45

LET'S HEAR IT FOR AUNTY LOL

◆

The Earth Hums in B Flat
by Mari Strachan
(2009)

I don't listen to many podcasts, but one favourite is *Backlisted*, which focuses each month on a book chosen by a literary guest that is usually not recently published and that they feel should be better known. Over the last decade, it's helped me choose what to read next, nudging me politely towards the likes of *Memento Mori* by Muriel Spark and Paula Fox's *Desperate Characters*. It's another *Backlisted* recommendation, *The Vet's Daughter* by Barbara Comyns – a story set in Edwardian London, a girl who discovers that she can levitate (coincidentally, this was an idea that Comyns came up with while on honeymoon in Wales) – that I am reminded of when I read the opening paragraph in *The Earth Hums in B Flat* by Mari Strachan:

> I fly in my sleep every night. When I was little I could fly without being asleep; now I can't, even though I practise and practise. And after what I saw last night I want more than ever to fly wide-awake. Mam always says; I want never gets. Is that true?

It is also one of the most intriguing starts to a book I've come across.

Gwenni Morgan is a charming but unusual twelve-year-old girl living in a small town in Wales in the late 1950s with her not-very-nice older sister, her increasingly unstable mother and her absolutely delightful father. The counterbalance to this difficult home life is Gwenni's highly imaginative worldview. Faces in the wallpaper talk to her, and the toby jugs on her mantlepiece have a life of their own. She believes she can fly. She is also the first-person narrator, which is all a little unsettling, as Gwenni has a shaky grasp of social norms. What starts off as a domestic family drama suddenly pivots into a complex detective story when a violent local shepherd disappears and all kinds of secrets in the town come to light.

The book covers many themes. You could sum it up as a study of congenital mental illness, domestic abuse, depression and illicit affairs. Or if you're more of a glass-half-full kind of person, it could be viewed as a portrait of loving fatherhood, a hymn to unconventionality and a celebration of the redemptive power of art and books.

Anyway, to give you some kind of idea of the notetaking I made while reading the books on the Welshly list, here are the disjointed thoughts I jotted down as I moved through the book (well, the ones I can decipher anyway) while I was reading it:

> Gwenni knows a lot more than she thinks she does
>
> *The Yellow Wallpaper*? *To Kill a Mockingbird*?
>
> Welsh is the key language – you don't know if they're talking Welsh or English until somebody says 'stop talking in Welsh'
>
> Little girl Gwenni babysits [and] complains about lack of books set in Wales. 'I wish I had stories about here, and not about old England'

Cleese and *Two Ronnies* sketch about class
Shows not tells
Coming of age story about not/nearly coming of
    age?
Does she actually fly? Not a stupid question.
    Magical realism? She definitely does *something*.
    Astral projection?
Gwenni reads Margery Allingham's *The Tiger in
    the Smoke*? Check.
Who knows where the time goes?

To be honest, I'm not sure why I wrote that last one as, on reflection, it doesn't seem at all applicable. I was probably just in one of my mournful, reflective states at the time. Anyway, the rest of the notes:

> So many great quotable bits. 'Alwenna says that
> Mr Williams winds his wife up every morning;
> she says you can tell by the way Mrs Williams talks
> more slowly in the afternoons and has nothing at
> all to say by evening. When I told Mam she said:
> Don't be silly, Gwenni.'
>   If Jacqueline Wilson wrote *One Moonlit Night*?
>   Quirky but not annoying – toby jugs thing
> could be cringy but actually very effective

I don't know about you, but usually when I read a book I don't take notes or even add my own pithy thoughts in the margins. But I might start because it's an interesting record of the thoughts that strike you at the time of reading, which might easily be forgotten later, even if some of them appear a bit random. I certainly would not have remembered to put Margery Allingham's *The Tiger in the Smoke* onto my TBR pile without this recorded nudge.

This is Strachan's first novel, published when she was sixty-one. It is also notable for making a memorable addition to the list of literature's finest unseen characters, which include Jane Gallagher in *The Catcher in the Rye*, and the expected Godot in Samuel Beckett's play. Gwenni's Aunty Lol, although we never meet her, is a presence in the book and it's always a pleasure to hear about what she's up to, whether that's playing trumpet in the town's brass band or turning out for the local women's football team. She's also a fantastic whistler thanks to the gap between her front teeth. Auntie Lol lends Gwenni detective stories, including *The Maltese Falcon*, and keeps an allotment, as well as a budgie called Lloyd George. If Gwenni's life is sometimes quite uninviting, at least she's always got Lol to fall back on.

Why this book matters... it shows the consequences of keeping secrets.

Read it because... there's a captivating feeling of not quite knowing what's going on even when you think you're ahead of the game.

Give it a miss if... you don't like mysteries.

What I discovered about Wales... it's possible to write in English but give the reader the feeling that they're reading and understanding Welsh.

BOOK 46

NANO-SYNAPTIC DREAM TABLETS

◆

The Meat Tree
by Gwyneth Lewis
(2010)

Throughout my Welshly quest, I continued to ask friends and other folk to recommend books for inclusion. I'll be honest, most of their suggestions weren't much help but, at this point in the game with the referee beginning to check his watch, a colleague came up with a very pertinent observation. 'You've not,' he said, 'included any science fiction.'

I hadn't even considered that there was any Welsh science fiction, which is very much my bad considering that said colleague immediately pointed out that Terry Nation (writer of old *Doctor Who*, *Survivors*, *Blake's Seven*) was from Cardiff, and that new *Doctor Who*'s Russell T Davies is from Swansea, before going on to name several other Welsh sci-fi writers and books. The one which sounded most interesting was *The Meat Tree* by Gwyneth Lewis.

The year is 2210, about fifty years before Captain Kirk and Spock are boldly roving the galaxy in the original television series of *Star Trek*. There's not a lot of scene-setting, but writers Robert Graves and Mircea Eliade and sculptor Henry Moore all get early namechecks so it was nice to see they have not been forgotten more than two centuries down the line. Nonetheless, things have moved on a bit since 2010, which is when this book was published, although the evergreen story of a grizzled old-timer who follows the rules and is coming back for one last job only to be paired with an ambitious young partner who wants to tear the rule book up is still with us. The flowery-named Campion is an Inspector of Wrecks who has spent a lifetime clearing up intergalactic spaceships that have come a serious cropper. When Campion finally retires, his bosses plan to replace him with robots. Nona is his younger apprentice who is keen to get the latest mission over with and head home. The name Nona comes from the Latin meaning ninth and is the name of one of the three Fates who was connected to destiny and childbirth, something which becomes increasingly relevant to the story.

Sent to, what initially appears to be, a normal if strangely unmanned vessel in space known to be home to a crew of three, Campion and Nona come across not only an obsolete cassette tape player but also a kind of advanced virtual reality role-playing game. It's even more sophisticated than the one the *Red Dwarf* crew find themselves in during the episode 'Back to Reality' if you can imagine that. But this game focuses on the medieval tale of the fourth branch of the *Mabinogion* – the same story that Alan Garner found inspiring for *The Owl Service*. Yep, despite not including the *Mab* in this book, I'm still nibbling away at it from various angles by accident.

The Meat Tree is part of publisher Seren's series of modern retellings of the *Mabinogion*. The list of writers who have contributed other volumes to it reads like a who's who of the Welshly list (if I may put it in such self-congratulatory terms), including Owen Sheers, Niall Griffiths, Trezza Azzopardi, Cynan Jones, Horatio Clare and Fflur Dafydd. As series editor Penny Thomas says in the introduction, 'Some stories, it seems, just keep on going. Whatever you do to them, the words are still whispered abroad.'

Lewis helpfully includes a brief summary of the original story of Blodeuwedd, which is hard to sum up in a few words but involves a family of warring, storytelling Welsh wizards, a woman created out of flowers, and that eponymous tree of meat. It's quite as peculiar as it sounds – perhaps it really should be shelved in the science fiction section, if shelving is your thing – but also very intriguing, and the two-hander narrative approach of the book raises plenty of questions about the motivation of all the characters involved.

Lacking a narrator, Campion and Nona provide a very detailed exposition of their journey through the game and what's going on, either through dialogue via a kind of psychic thought-sharing application (ah, the white heat of *Jetsons* technology) or through their internal thoughts. Each time they enter the game, they take a different part – switching between male and female identities – in the belief that the truth about the mystery of the crew's absence is somehow embedded in the game. Since the story from the *Mabinogion* involves rape, incest, bestiality, adultery, murder and shape-shifting and, given that virtual reality in this world has advanced considerably since the days of the quaint twenty-first-century Oculus headset, it's quite a bruising experience for both of them. And for the reader it's not just *what's* going on, but *who's* going on.

I'm only an occasional sci-fi reader, but sometimes the exposition seemed a little heavy-handed in *The Meat Tree*. That, coupled with the occasional technochat with its nano-synaptic dream tablets, Microscopium Void, and so forth left me a bit cold. Also, I'm not convinced that anybody in 2210 will be using such antiquated terms as "Atta girl!' and 'Hark at you!'. Campion is a fuddy-duddy jobsworth with a smack of Kenneth Williams's campness.

Yet Lewis brings something very fresh to the game. She was the first National Poet of Wales, so as you might expect, the language is extremely lyrical (not that all sci-fi has to be purely commercial shoot-'em-up-cowboys versus aliens-in-space stuff before the angry letters of protest pour in to the publisher). Her afterword makes clear that this is a book about imagination and an acknowledgements list that thanks Maurice Maeterlinck's *The Intelligence of Flowers* Charles Darwin's *The Power of Movement in Plants* and the likes of Philip Robert Harris's *Living and Working in Space: Human Behaviour, Culture and Organisation* underlines that she is offering an intriguing take on the original ancient *Mabinogion* myth. What's also interesting is that, even though this book was written relatively recently, technology as is its wont has hurtled forward and we are now in the age of artificial intelligence.

While, in a sense, the puzzle is resolved in the final pages, an absolutely key part of the whole conundrum is *not* explained and the reader is left to provide their own answer. It would be a really poor show to reveal anything about the ending of this interstellar *Marie Celeste* story, but I will say that it looks at the blurring of biological boundaries, is thought-provoking and will certainly provide ample fodder for book clubs to mull over. It would also make a fabulous graphic novel.

Why this book matters... it puts you off playing video games.

Read it because... it will encourage you to read the Mabinogion.

Give it a miss if... you didn't like Stanislaw Lem's *Solaris* or Arthur C. Clarke's *2001: A Space Odyssey*.

What I discovered about Wales... its literary tentacles can reach far into time and space.

BOOK 47

A BLOW TO THE HEAD

◆

The Dig
by Cynan Jones
(2014)

Although I'm usually quite grumpy about anything I regard as overly self-indulgent or navel-gazing, after I finished this novel about badger-baiting, I sat in my chair and thought for a while about why I read it. Indeed, I had paused briefly to ponder the same topic after reaching... (checks note) page five of the book. And I don't think that's something I have ever done before. I've always liked reading, but beyond the obvious motivations to read – such as to pass exams or humblebrag about my end-of-year 'What I Read' list – *why* I do it has remained part of my unexamined life.

There are, of course, certain mental health benefits connected to reading: improved emotional intelligence, delaying the onset of dementia, higher self-esteem and even better sleep. I can't really say any of these are why *I* read. They're nice by-products, yes. But main motivation? No.

One reason I read is to find illumination about the world around me. When I look back over the last half a dozen years of reading, non-fiction books such as *Black Tudors* by Miranda Kaufmann, *Islander: A Journey Around our Archipelago* by Patrick Barkham, and *Underland* by Robert Macfarlane, have been some of my most enjoyable reads. To paraphrase Dr Seuss: reading takes you to fascinating places. And the main reason I pick out certain fiction is simply that something about the subject appeals to me, whether that's the blokey nostalgia of Andrew O'Hagan's *Mayflies* or the imagined future of Kim Stanley Robinson's *Red Mars*. My process is far more random when it comes to poetry. I usually pick a collection based on the strength of seeing a stanza, or sometimes just a line or two, in a review and this has brought me gems such as Carole Bromley's poetry collection *The Peregrine Falcons of York Minster*. I tend to pick poetry less for subject matter and more because I like the style of the writing. So I think I read to make myself think, whether that's very specifically about something with a title like *How to Live: A life of Montaigne* by Sarah Bakewell, or more generally with something like *The Gap in the Curtain* by John Buchan.

On this premise, I felt obliged to persevere with *The Dig* since I – as I suspect most other people living in suburbia – knew nothing about the world of badger-baiting and maybe the book would enlarge my mind.

In *The Dig*, an unnamed menacing 'big man' digs out badgers from their setts and then unflinchingly pits them against dogs for a paying audience. Meanwhile, living nearby is Daniel, who is trying to cope with a domestic tragedy on his west Wales sheep farm in Ceredigion. Both situations are told in alternating sections and paragraphs, with graphic fight scenes and intense personal introspection. Inevitably, the two men's lives overlap. Although in the most basic sense, *The Dig* is about badger-baiting, it's fundamentally a meditation on death, the often harsh reality of rural life and the fragile nature of safety. The ending to this grim 160-page work of rural gothic is particularly fine. Written in a blunt, restrained style that matches the subdued black-and-white of my edition's cover design and prompted strong memories of reading *Martha, Jack & Shanco*, it is not a book that you will forget. That said, if you find animal cruelty difficult to read about, give this the widest of berths.

Another thought that crossed my mind as I turned the last raw page of *The Dig* was that I read because I *like* what I'm reading. As Vladimir Nabokov said: 'Knowing you have something good to read before bed is among the most pleasurable of sensations.'[2] That is very much my view. I don't mind something emotionally intense, but what I'm not after is something that will disturb me. That's what floated Franz Kafka's boat. In a letter to his friend Oskar Pollak in 1904 he argued that people should only read books that wounded or stabbed them, things that woke them up like a blow to the head; otherwise what's the point of reading? Perhaps I'm shallow, but I am not looking for my book to maim me.

So, I'm glad I read *The Dig*. I'm probably a better person for having done so, even though I frequently winced along the journey. But I'm also glad I'm not going to read it again.

Why this book matters... it shows how you can carry on with life when something awful happens to you.

Read it because... the good people end happily(ish) and the bad people end unhappily(ish).

Give it a miss if... you don't want to read about animal cruelty.

What I discovered about Wales... too much information about what happens in badger-baiting.

2 www.life.com/animals/vladimir-nabokov-and-his-butterflies-photos/#1

BOOK 48

ENGLISH IS SLUDGY

◆

Pigeon
by Alys Conran
(2016)

From a book that was something of a battle to pick up to one that I found hard to put down. Actually, I don't think I *did* put it down, as I read it in one sitting on a train from London to York. I read the first page while I was hanging around in King's Cross Station and then finished it off in the York Tap pub at my destination after I arrived. When I was younger, I used to do this more frequently. I remember reading through the night to finish Umberto Eco's *The Name of the Rose* as a student and walking around Wellington in New Zealand with my finger as a bookmark in *Miss Smilla's Feeling for Snow* by Peter Høeg so that I could carry on reading while waiting at road crossings. I hardly do it at all now. New *Asterix* adventures are about the only length I can cope with in a single gulp.

Pigeon is also one of those books that starts off in one direction and then veers away sharply. Sylvia Townsend Warner does that remarkably well in *Lolly Willowes or the Loving Huntsman* – a story of late-life liberation that suddenly does a handbrake turn into a date with the Devil. *Pigeon* starts off as a coming-of-age tale in a Welsh village (possibly Bethesda, the setting for *One Moonlit Night* with which it shares the themes of mental stability, chapel life and childhood poverty) and becomes something much darker and more mysterious.

When the twist comes, it's a cracker. As soon as I finished the book, I went straight back to reread the pivotal passage, which had seemed straightforward at the time. It's one of those moments when you're reading and say to yourself, 'Hey, hang on, that's not what happened,' and then when you flick backwards to check your own memory, it all becomes obvious. That said, there's no 'look how clever I am' posturing here, and it's all the more readable and real for it. It's a marvellously clever piece of storytelling written in a very straightforward style.

The two leads are 1990s schoolfriends Iola Williams and the eponymous Pigeon, who muck about together, make up weird stories about the local ice cream seller, and try to make the best of their imperfect family lives. Their stories scurry out of control. Pigeon's home life takes a major turn for the worse, and the innocence of their childhoods is obliterated as time passes. Both the characters are engaging in very different ways. Iola is technically the lively heroine of the piece. Pigeon, I'd have to say, is closer to the shady anti-hero end of the spectrum. He's a kind of overlooked juvenile everyman (hence his ubiquitous bird name). It wouldn't be quite right to think of them as Cathy and Heathcliff but that coupling did nag at me several times while I was reading. You still root for Pigeon and hope he gets out the other end ok. It's by no means certain that this will happen.

Of course, words matter in all the Welshly books, and language is absolutely central to Conran's work. It was, in a world first, published simultaneously by Parthian in both English and as *Pijin* in a Welsh translation by Sian Northey. As I've previously confessed, I'm not knowledgeable enough to comment on the Welsh text, but I would say this is a textbook example of how to write characters speaking in a non-English language without alienating the English-speaking readership. Conran – whose father Tony taught both my parents English at Bangor University (they remember him fondly)

– does this very neatly. Welsh is the characters' first language, and quite often Welsh words slip in among the English – more often, I'm sure, than in anything else I've read so far. When this happens, a translation is indicated and sometimes the next line or two makes it clear what they've been saying. Sometimes, though, there's no help at all, but at no point was I left flummoxed. In fact, at these points I felt flattered that the author was involving me, and relying on my having enough grey matter to work out what was being said without recourse to a Welsh dictionary. How Sian Northey managed this in reverse, effectively translating what is already a Welsh book into Welsh, would be fascinating to get to grips with. Maybe I'll get there one day.

What the Welsh language means to the two best friends becomes very clear in the part of the book where Pigeon – whose unexpectedly sensuous delight in wordplay has earlier confounded any classist expectations about who words are for – decides to abandon it in favour of English. There are good reasons for this, but Iola, who believes 'English is sludgy', is incredulous. Again, Pigeon's motives for the language loss are not hammered home with a mallet but merely neatly underlined.

Why this book matters… the two epigraphs at the beginning of the story are wisely chosen.

Read it because… it twists and turns in directions you can't foresee.

Give it a miss if… you find child abuse triggering.

What I discovered about Wales… it presents another link in the chain to establish the importance of the Welsh language to identity.

BOOK 49

CARNAL LUST

◆

Water Shall Refuse Them
by Lucie McKnight Hardy
(2019)

This slice of folk horror is set in the summer drought of 1976.
I was in primary school back then, gasping during a sponsored
walk on a roasting hot day, younger than the sixteen-year-old
first-person narrator, Nif, but older than her little brother, Lorry.
I haven't thought about that summer much over the last half a
century, but this languid account of an English family looking to
get itself back on track in Wales during a month in the country
brought it shimmering back. *Water Shall Refuse Them* is a creepy
folk-tale set in the Welsh countryside with its trademark rural
locations, odd local customs, inward-looking residents and
unwitting incomers.

It gets off to an appropriately Gothic start with mum, dad, Nif,
and Lorry heading, with hope in their hearts, towards a friend's
holiday home. In a very off-putting beginning, Nif is holding a
head in her lap during the car journey. I had to reread the first
few pages to make sure I hadn't misread that. Nope, it's a head.
It's a while before this is explained, but in the meantime, it's
creepy – not misty castles-creepy or *Scooby Doo*-creepy, but it's
obvious very early on that things are not going well and that life
is not looking likely to perk up.

The cause of the melancholy is the accidental death of Lorry's twin sister during a routine bath some months earlier. Nif and Lorry seem to be coping ok. She acts like a second mother to her brother – well, most of the time. Their dad is naturally grieving though struggling on. But their mum is in bits. The plan is to spend the summer in Wales – believing that getting away from it all for a while will help her deal with her grief. However, when they turn up at their new temporary home, they find a village with unnerving neighbours, including a church congregation who are immediately at odds with them and a sensuous and distinctly witchy woman, Janet, and her odd teenage son, Mally. Mally is, it is explained, short for Malcolm, but it harks back to the epigraph, which is a quote from the famous witchcraft treatise the *Malleus Maleficarum*: 'All witchcraft comes from carnal lust, which in women is insatiable.'

Although it's a scorcher, Nif observes that: 'There's a special time of day, when light is caught in limbo. Dusk: that time when the twilight dips to a level where light and dark start to merge, and everything takes on a silvery, ghost-like sheen, when it's difficult to tell where one thing ends and another begins, and the lines of things are all blurred together.' The action takes place through this haze, progressing at a gentle trot through the energy-sapping heat of the summer – that is, until the last few pages when it suddenly gallops along at full speed and careers into a properly disquieting ending. That isn't to say that it's all picnics in the back garden and walks on the beach before that. There's horror aplenty, but it's more the kind of gnawing suspense found in Iain Banks's *The Wasp Factory* or Shirley Jackson's *We Have Always Lived in the Castle*. It also took me back to some worrying moments of reading Michelle Paver's *Dark Matter*.

There are plenty of unnerving moments. When the newly arrived family optimistically visit the local pub – another of those staples in rural horror stories – they accidentally intrude on a meeting of some of the church congregation in a back room. While it's not clear what the meeting is about, the family are politely but firmly ushered out. We never find out what the meeting is about, which is, in itself not a huge deal, but these little unexplained events of the story keep adding up until there's a cocktail of disquiet sloshing around.

'When men choose not to believe in God, they do not thereafter believe in nothing. They then become capable of believing in anything,' wrote Belgian playwright Émile Cammaerts (not G. K. Chesterton, as is often suggested). This is certainly true here. Nif's lapsed-Catholic mother, Linda, happily latches on to witchy neighbour Janet's alternative and pagan approach to life. Nif develops several self-help rituals, which she calls the Creed, to try and bring a balance to her own life. Mally has his own series of sacraments that he plays close to his chest. Even the villagers seem to have adopted some ad hoc inventions of their own into their pious religious practice. Like witch hunts. Some of what the people in the novel do in the name of their beliefs to empower themselves is a bit odd. Some of it is just nauseating, and there is some really unpleasant animal as well as human cruelty. Anybody who has a soft spot for squirrels, of any colour, will not enjoy this book.

Why this book matters... it shows you can still have a riveting read and leave some loose ends for the reader to ponder.

Read it because... it really captures that meteorological experience of the drought of 1976.

Give it a miss if... you are not a fan of horror fiction.

What I discovered about Wales... I realise it sounds ridiculous, but I hadn't really grasped that it got so hot there too.

BOOK 50

O! WHAT A LOVELY WAR

◆

The Gododdin: Lament for the Fallen
by Gillian Clarke
(2021)

'Lament' is not the word I'd have used to describe this account of a seventh-century battle between a Scottish tribe and the Germanic Angles that ended in a massacre in North Yorkshire. (You might already be thinking 'Welsh' is another descriptor that seems inappropriate, but we'll come to that in a minute.)

For me, a lament is W. H. Auden's 'Funeral Blues', Louis Armstrong singing 'Nobody Knows the Trouble I've Seen', or Frank Sinatra moping in 'The Wee Small Hours of the Morning'. *The Gododdin* is much more sprightly than these. It's more like 'Adelaide's Lament' from *Guys and Dolls* than Purcell's final aria for Dido as she contemplates stabbing herself for the love of Aeneas: 'Remember me, but ah! forget my fate.' No, *The Gododdin* (or *Y Gododdin* as it is in the original old Welsh) is a full-on glorification of a heavy-drinking, belligerent brotherhood who slaughtered, kamikaze-style, anything in their path on the field of war. This is an account of the Battle of Thermopylae set in Catterick. Reet, lads, prepare for glory!

The start of an appreciation for the model warrior called Cydywal emphasises that he could take his drink, was astonishing in battle, and left plenty of carrion corpses for the birdlife to feast on. Cydywal's write-up is fairly typical of the hagiographic style of the poem, which dates back to around a hundred years after the Battle of Catraeth, a clash between a Celtic tribe known as the Gododdin, who came up against the far superior force of invading Angles. Initially an oral composition meant to be sung or recited, it was written down around the seventh century by the Welsh poet Aneirin and is here translated for a modern audience by Gillian Clarke, whom we have already met on the Welshly list. The manuscript version that has come down to us today dates from the thirteenth century and tells how only a single lucky soldier, or sometimes three since the count in the poem varies, returned from the fray of a total of 300.

Gillian Clarke's winning new translation begins with a *Beowulf*-style address to the reader set in the traditional mead-hall surroundings with a continuously roaring fire and a big crowd who are up for some entertainment and equally happy to welcome in sociable strangers. Although the battle ended in a near total annihilation, as Aneirin sets off on his epic, he puts the best possible shine on things, reminding me of Japanese Emperor Hirohito's pronouncement to the nation in August 1945 in the wake of Japan's defeat and the nuclear destruction of two of its cities. He remarked that 'the war situation has developed not necessarily to Japan's advantage.' He explains how the soldiers geared themselves up for the war, which seems to be through a year-long pub crawl. To me, the son of Quakers, this does not sound like a wise move.

Aneirin's poem is not a narrative. The poem is more like an extended memorial of the war, with Aneirin selecting a chosen few big names from Team Gododdin and providing edited career highlights. Each man's life is covered in a few lines, with some repetitive themes. Lots of them delight in flashing their jewellery and their golden armour. And they also revel in Oliver Reed-levels of drinking mead, though this is less boozy than it looks at first sight as the meaning of 'mead' is fluid in the piece and references both the amber nectar and more general human qualities such as loyalty. There's no solid detail about what happened during the battle or even why the Gododdin came such a cropper, it's simply a veneration of the participants and an early exemplar of how to be a good loser. While it naturally focuses on the soldiers' fighting capacity, there are also some nice little other human touches. Gwenabwy is one that stands out. He should not be forgotten, says Aneirin, because not only did he never turn tail and flee, he always paid his minstrels and – I think this is a key comment on his character – gave them a whopping tip at the end of the year.

This is also arguably one of the first times the legend of King Arthur is namechecked in any literature. Very late on in the text, the bravery of one slaughtered fighter is measured, slightly unfavourably, against the kingpin of Camelot. There's also a very brief mention of Myrddin, a Welsh poet, who is better known to most of us as Merlin.

This is a marvellously flowing translation by Gillian Clarke with Welsh and English texts on opposite pages. Even if you can't read the Welsh (in Aneirin's day the Welsh language enjoyed a far wider geographic spread of everyday usage in Britain than it does now and even stretched to areas of what is now southern Scotland and Edinburgh), I think it's still worth spending some time on it and reading parts of it aloud as the words roll off the tongue quite beautifully. It's interesting that David Jones found inspiration from this text and began each of the sections of *In Parenthesis* (Book 2) with a quote from *The Gododdin*. Again, the closer I get to the end of the Welshly list, the more shapes and patterns I can see.

I realise it's a bit of a cheat to include something written a millennium and a half ago in a list supposedly culled from books published during the last century, but there's a real thrill in reading this twenty-first-century version. I love *Sir Gawain and the Green Knight*, a mere whippersnapper composed only in the fourteenth century and, in fact, I have a collection of various editions of it (the evenings fly by in our household). There are various reasons why I reread it so regularly, but one of them is the amazement at not just being able to enjoy something written so many centuries ago but also to be able to empathise with the action. *The Gododdin*, like Seamus Heaney's *Beowulf*, is not just one for the military buffs, it's one for anybody who loves poetry. And brandishing their brooches.

Why this book matters... it's kind of where Welsh literature starts.

Read it because... considering there's no plot and nothing happens, it bounces along in a very engaging way.

Give it a miss if... you find the glorification of war distasteful.

What I discovered about Wales... the geographic extent of the Celtic language in medieval times.

BOOK 51

IT'S THE END
OF THE WORLD
AS WE KNOW IT

◆

The Blue Book of Nebo
by Manon Steffan Ros
(2022)

◆

previously published in Welsh as *Llyfr Glas Nebo* (2018)

I am a big fan of novels that aren't shouty, like *The Beginning of Spring* by Penelope Fitzgerald, J. L. Carr's *A Month in the Country* or pretty much anything by Angela Thirkell. Even when serious topics and important relationships are under the microscope, it doesn't mean a writer can't be a little understated and gently elliptical. A skilled author can lightly demand attention rather than being right up in the reader's face all the time. I understand that this is much harder to do when the subject matter is the near-destruction of civilisation, though. Yet, where the focus of Cormac McCarthy's gloomy *The Road* is on the downside of a post-apocalyptic world peopled by cannibals, Manon Steffan Ros shows that it is possible to take a more upbeat approach to what she labels 'The End'.

The eponymous blue book is a joint diary kept by mother and son Rowenna and Dylan, written eight years after something unidentified but definitely *very* bad happens to the world. The diary offers us their alternating views of survival in the face of almost total disaster in the small northwest Welsh town of Nebo. Enigmatically, the bad stuff went down in 2018 and the main body of the action is set in that year, which means it's the only post-apocalyptic novel set in the past/present I can think of. (How about you?) For thirty-six-year-old Rowenna, who remembers what life was like before the presumed nuclear curtain came almost all the way down, it's a constant battle against the odds as she faces living, horror of horrors, 'without the radio, Snapchat and Facebook'. But for fourteen-year-old Dylan, who remembers almost nothing of what happened eight years ago, life is good, even if it is a bit on the solitary side without any other humans around except his mother and baby sister, Mona. There is a particularly touching moment when he finds himself becoming slightly obsessed with a photo of a teenage girl in one of the abandoned houses he explores. Dylan's also a bit of a whizz on the agricultural side of things meaning that, in some ways, this is a fictional companion to some of the farming memoirs from earlier on the list. Dylan works hard and appreciates the simple things in life and the self-sufficient nature of their existence. For his birthday, he asks for a conservatory. Or rather, he asks for permission from his mother to build his own conservatory. Together, mother and son certainly make a better, more uplifting fist of things than the much harder-to-like family in the more Hollywood post-disaster novel *Leave the World Behind* by Rumaan Alam, which I read in parallel to this in a week and lacked similar laughs.

The Blue Book of Nebo leans more towards the measured bleakness J. G. Ballard's characters enjoy in his meteorologically dystopian novels *The Drowned World* and *The Burning World* – things may have gone badly wrong, but there's still something to be said for carrying on regardless. Eventually, Rowenna finds her son's eternal optimism infectious, especially his love of language and the joy he takes in his native Welsh tongue. He fires off quotes from his extensive reading like Hector's pupils in Alan Bennett's *The History Boys*, with the result that my Welshly list has extended beyond the remit of this book, and I will be checking out the *Black Book of Carmarthen*, the *Red Book of Hergest*, *Lladd Duw* by Dewi Prysor, and *Y Gymydd* by Caryl Lewis. Dylan's wide-eyed interest in the world of print extends to an interest in the Bible, which prompts thoughts that we're locked into some kind of modern parable equivalent to Noah's flood. For Rowenna, his enthusiasm offers her a chance to reconnect with her cultural roots, though she's less keen on going back to anything theological.

Interestingly, the English edition I read is a translation by Steffan Ros, who grew up in Eryri, north Wales, and was regularly taken on CND marches as a child. Her original Welsh version of the story *Llyfr Glas Nebo* was published a couple of years earlier. As with some of the other books in translation I've tackled, it's really annoying that my Welsh isn't good enough (yet) to have a go at the original because the author says that the theme of language is stronger in the English than the Welsh version. In an interview with the online community United by Pop, she commented: 'There's more of an examination of what it means to your identity when you speak a minority language, and about the idea that there's a right way and a wrong way to speak, write or experience a language.'

I enjoyed Emily St John Mandel's *Station Eleven* very much as I did both the television series and the novelisation of Terry Nation's *Survivors*, but they are both stuffed full of packs of out-of-control goons roaming the countryside. There's virtually nobody else at all in deserted post-disaster Nebo. While there is peril, such as radiation sickness and mutant fauna, and everyday life is tough with no power – and worst of all no social media – there is also hope. *The Blue Book of Nebo* also has an unexpected and genre-busting ending that doesn't leave you crying into your wine. It's also been marketed as a crossover book and rightly won a Carnegie Award. If you're put off by the Young Adult label, then let me assure you that it felt to me more like the kind of short but sensitive novel that put me in mind of Claire Keegan's fine work.

Why this book matters... it might help you reassess the really important things in life for you and your loved ones.

Read it because... it's oddly comforting to read a post-apocalypse novel that feels banally realistic.

Give it a miss if... you're fond of Porthmadog, which does not have a great apocalypse.

What I discovered about Wales... 'instinct makes you save that which you're most in danger of losing.' (Rowenna, page 47, Firefly Press, paperback edition).

BOOK 52

UNDER THE MOON OF LOVE

◆

My Family and Other Rock Stars
by *Tiffany Murray*
(2024)

So here we are, book 52, the end of the line. I left the choice for this last piece in the Welshly jigsaw until the very end and trusted fate to deliver something intriguing. I had numerous possibilities, but whittled the shortlist down to three. Missing out on the final squad collection was the historical eco-travelogue *Sarn Helen: A Journey Through Wales, Past, Present and Future* by Tom Bullough with illustrations by Jackie Morris, and *The Shadow Key*, a gothic novel set in Wales, by Susan Stokes-Chapman. I will definitely read both, and the novel is currently on the desk in front of me. But Tiffany Murray's culinary memoir pipped them to the post, partly because of its unique story but also because two separate friends in the book biz had mentioned it to – one before it was even published. They both told me it was not to be missed and, in some ways, they were right.

This is Murray's own story of growing up as the daughter of Joan, a cordon bleu chef to the pop stars who attended the famed Rockfield recording studio in Monmouthshire. As a child, Murray met and helped to feed many familiar names, including the likes of Queen, Black Sabbath, Motörhead, Showaddywaddy, Squeeze, Siouxsie Sioux, David Bowie (who seems not to eat very much at all) and Graham Parker (who has a fondness for scarfing trout). She watches in amazement as Ozzy Osbourne goes bananas in a graveyard in the middle of the night, and she bonds with Freddie Mercury over a shared love of dogs. Everybody seems remarkably polite and restrained, and a food fight between Simple Minds, Iggy Pop and David Bowie is about as high as the jinks get. No televisions were hurt in the making of this book.

Along the way, for those of us of a certain age who were also children in the 1970s, there are plenty of familiar names to stir our nostalgia, including books like *Fattypuffs and Thinifers*, television shows like *Crystal Tipps and Alistair* and *Tiswas* and the memory of Jimmy Osmond posters on bedroom walls. It's all done with plenty of brio and atmosphere. The 1976 drought that we saw wreaking emotional havoc in McKnight Hardy's *Water Shall Refuse Them*, here forced Joan to plunge herself into a string of cold baths to keep cool.

The memoir is written from the point of view of the infant Tiffany and covers her childhood from the age of nearly six to about thirteen, when she accidentally snogs a roadie. It's a kind of recreated diary, unless she has abnormal powers of recall or kept a spectacularly detailed journal. There are also foodie snippets in the form of recipes, and an additional parental perspective on matters from her no-nonsense mother, and some other brief diary extracts about which bands are in situ (the author of these is, slightly confusingly, not really explained). It actually reads more like fiction – indeed Murray's first novel, *Diamond Star Halo*, was partly inspired by her childhood. And, really, what does it matter what we call it since it is tremendously engaging, from Lemmy's obsession with bacon sandwiches to the dreadful realisation that zebra finches and Steradent don't mix. At all.

But on the downside, it's not about Wales in any real sense. Ella Risbridger describes it on the front cover as 'a *Hideous Kinky* for Wales', which it really is not. Patrick Gale's comparison to *Cider with Rosie* on the back cover is much more apt. Apart from a visit to a second-hand bookshop in Llandrindod Wells and a record shop in Monmouth, Cymru is absent. This is not the book's fault. It never promises large servings of Welshness, but I'd just assumed that there would be an ample menu of it. So, in a fairly basic way, it means it's rather an anti-climax to the list. But wearing my glass-half-full hat, while there's no exploration of Welsh identity, it does mark a time in the recording industry when eyes were on the country as some of the biggest names in music descended on a farm in Wales to create timeless masterpieces. I certainly don't regret having read it and it's left me with warm feelings towards the whole Welshly enterprise.

Why this book matters... it shows a down-to-earth human side to legendary figures more familiar from the pages of tabloids.

Read it because... it will make you happy and probably hungry.

Give it a miss if... stories about pop stars mucking around a bit leave you cold.

What I discovered about Wales... Wye salmon sounds tempting.

CONCLUSION:
They think it's all over

The same year that John Lubbock suggested his top hundred reads, Oscar Wilde also offered his two-pennies-worth in a letter to *The Pall Mall Gazette* in which he outlined three classes of book. The first section contained books he recommended we should all read, such as Vasari's *Lives of the Artists* and Cicero's letters. The second were those to reread and included Plato and Keats, who were, in Wilde's own enigmatic words, 'in the sphere of poetry, the masters not the minstrels; in the sphere of philosophy, the seers not the *savants*'. His third list was of books not to read at all – suggesting it's best to steer well clear of all Voltaire's plays, and 'all argumentative books and all books that try to prove anything'. And Wilde finishes by arguing that: 'The third class is by far the most important. To tell people what to read is, as a rule, either useless or harmful; for, the appreciation of literature is a question of temperament not of teaching.'

I hope that even if you've found this book useless, it hasn't actually harmed you. It certainly hasn't injured me. Quite the reverse, I'm modestly proud of myself for not only finishing it, but enjoying the process. Even the titles I can't say I warmed to were still stimulating and took me out of my reading comfort zone – a place I usually like to hang around in a lot. Even if *The Old Devils* was like watching England play in the Euros 2024 – several hours of my life I'll never get back. I'm still miffed with Kingsley about that. But it's a small price to pay for what feels like an itch partially scratched, even if it's an itch that I actually hope will continue to give me pleasure for many years to come. Along the way, we've moved from the impact of Darwinian theory, to the coming of the railways, through two world wars and the reconstruction of Cardiff's Tiger Bay, before coming *very* close to the end of the world in north Wales. The Welshly list has also shimmied back to the seventh century and even managed to include some science fiction. After a year and fifty-two books (plus a couple of diversionary ones that didn't get their own chapters) I'd never try to argue that I've mastered the whole of Welsh literature and gained a comprehensive view of the Welsh psyche, but it's a decent start on improving my previous ignorance. And I'm keen to go further – as I've mentioned numerous times, improving my spoken Welsh is also on the cards.

One regret is that there's been virtually nothing about music in the list. It feels like a major omission considering the country is so famous for being adept at singing, playing and performing music. The final book notwithstanding, I should have made more of an effort to track something down about Wales's relationship with music, especially as this book was largely written with music playing in the background. To go some way to make up for this absence I've put together a *My Year of Reading Welshly* playlist on Spotify, which features plenty of Welsh music and composers. If you would like to listen then search 'My Year of Reading Welshly' on Spotify playlists.

There's also very little about food – something I'm very, perhaps too, fond of – on the list. It would have added a different dimension to have included something like Carwyn Graves's *Welsh Food Stories* or Elizabeth Luard's 2011 *A Cook's Year in a Welsh Farmhouse*, (not least because my distinguished cookery writer friend Mark Diacono loves it, but also because it features a Welsh winter *cawl*, which I could have enjoyed as I was coming to the end of the list).

The Welshly experience has also helped me to reflect on *how* and *what* I read so, in a wider sense, it's been well worth it. And if the Welshly list in any way encourages you to pick up any of the books I read or ones I have mentioned in passing, then I'll be very happy. People – and I include myself in this huge generalisation – don't read enough or widely enough and the more helpful prods we can give each other the better. Having said that, whatever you read and however you read it, you should enjoy the experience. If it turns out that the *Mabinogion* isn't your *paned o de* (cup of tea), don't feel bad, just pick something else. You can always come back to it another time – or not, as the fancy takes you.

For what it's worth, my five favourite reads, in no particular order, were:

+ *Border Country* by Raymond Williams (Book 11)
+ *Jampot Smith* by Jeremy Brooks (Book 12)
+ *One Moonlit Night* Caradog Prichard (Book 14)
+ *Travels with the Duchess* by Menna Gallie (Book 21)
+ *Five Pubs, Two Bars and a Nightclub* by John Williams (Book 34)

I think it's the poetry I'll come back to before any of those, though. It was the poetry on the list that made me pause for thought most frequently and had me noting down lines and couplets to pass off unattributed as my own wise words in the future.

In practical terms, I think fifty-two books, one after another, is too many in one year. I've overdosed and if I do something similar again, I'll spread it out a bit over more than a year, which would keep my momentum up but would stop me gazing wistfully at the shiny new books in my local bookshop and trying to work out if I could fit a little one in as an amuse-bouche. If you manage to read them all, I salute your vigour, especially if you do it in a year. If you read somewhere between one and fifty-two, congratulations on that, too. If you have got this far and haven't been tempted by anything, I apologise – but I do urge you to keep looking. There are so many Welsh books out there that I've not even touched on.

Here's Wilde again on his disappointment at the omissions in Lubbock's list: 'I am also amazed to find that Edgar Allan Poe has been passed over. Surely this marvellous lord of rhythmic expression deserves a place? If, in order to make room for him, it be necessary to elbow out someone else, I should elbow out Southey, and I think that Baudelaire might be most advantageously substituted for Keble.' And I admit that I feel a bit bad about all the marvellous books I didn't have space to shoehorn in. There are too many Welsh names missing from my list to mention. If I had the time again I think I would have thrown some more short stories into the mix, which would have added an extra Dolly Mixture to the big bag of treats.

It would also have been nice to have had someone to chat with about what I was reading. My wife is very patient and was open (well, fairly open) to me reading out choice bits from the Welshly list as I went along and we did talk about some of them in a general sense. Other friends and acquaintances also provided welcome thoughts, but a full-time Welshly co-reader would have been helpful. I think many of these books would work very well for reading groups where discussion can provide enlightenment.

I read in a mixture of my usual favourite places: in the bath, in bed, on the sofa, on the train, in the car waiting to pick up my children and at my parents' house. I ingested all of the list in traditional paper format with a bit of audio-visual thrown in for *Under Milk Wood*. Perhaps I'd try more audio books next time, but I'm not overly keen on ebooks. For me, there's so much joy in the physical feel of the book, the annotations and inclusions of previous owners of second-hand editions and the pleasure of looking at a spine on a shelf. Although, I suppose the pleasure of deleting *The Old Devils* off an e-reading device would have felt nice. I still feel some guilt over not finishing *The Book of Three* and I think I'll come back to it in the future to give it a full outing. I'm not a ruthless book discarder, honest.

On such a small and possibly unrepresentative selection of books I'm reluctant to make any sweeping generalisations about what I've learned, but it's important to look at what my armchair bookpacking around the country taught me about Wales. In a basic sense, I've extended my Welsh vocabulary in a way, which was thankfully more diverting than many of my online lessons. And I've also extended my knowledge of some aspects of the country's history. I could have got both of these by adding a couple of history books but novels, poems, memoirs and travelogues can be effective springboards for finding out more about the true nuts and bolts of how a place has been put together and how it is continuing to put itself together. The experience has made Wales much more three-dimensional for me and added a degree of depth to how I view the country and its people. I won't look at a map of it again without resonances about everyday life, work and poverty from the pages of these books sounding in my mind.

I think it's obvious that there has been a repeated and increasing emphasis on the centrality of the Welsh language to Welsh identity. Where the Welsh language was barely even referred to in the earlier books on the list, it became a central theme to almost all the later ones, which evidences its resurgence after hovering worryingly in the endangered zone for some time. What's also changed as we moved through the years is the subject matter. It became much darker, perhaps more nuanced, but certainly a lot more explicit and serious – some would argue that it's become a lot more realistic as we moved away from the cosiness of *Under Milk Wood*. It's not all fun and games in *How Green Was My Valley* or *The Battle to the Weak* but they seem like gentle stories for children in comparison to *Grits* and *The Dig*. The later books also managed to feel less insular and yet prouder of the Welsh language, history and culture at the same time. Survival is perhaps the overriding theme of all the books on the list, even if it's less dramatically at the fore for some titles than it is in *Brothers* and *Resistance*. Also of note is that, from the earliest titles onwards, youth's dissatisfaction with the status quo is a constant. From Esther in *The Battle to the Weak* to Nona far in the future in *The Meat Tree*, the younger generation are justifiably keen to make their own marks on the world or even to remake it in a better way. This healthy, positive desire of the young gives many of the books the kind of jet propulsion that is lacking in – sorry if it sounds like I've developed an obsessive downer on it – *The Old Devils*, which is very much a looking-back-in-anger book.

I've talked about the idea of piecing together a jigsaw a couple of times in these pages because that's how I've often felt as I gathered together such disparate and yet linked titles. At this point I feel like I've done most of the edges and filled in some small sections here and there, but I can see that there's hundreds more pieces before I have a whole picture of sky and mountains and buildings and people and sheep. I've had a look at the front of the box so I have some idea of how it should look. It just needs some time and patience.

So, what shall I read next?

BOOK CLUB
DISCUSSION QUESTIONS

◆

The Battle to the Weak by Hilda Vaughan
- How twentieth-century does the book feel, in style and substance?
- Does this book do for Radnorshire what the Brontës did for Yorkshire?
- Is Esther too much of a goody-two-shoes?
- Who is right about society, Esther or Rhys?

In Parenthesis by David Jones
- Would you describe this as a poem or a novel?
- How does it compare to other First World War poetry/novels you've read?
- Are the endnotes helpful?
- Would you find a rereading of it enlightening?

How Green Was My Valley by Richard Llewellyn
- Does Llewellyn's Welshness matter?
- Is this a Welsh *Cider with Rosie*?
- How would you rate the film version of the book?
- Does it feel like an unfinished story that requires sequels?

I Bought a Mountain by Thomas Firbank

- Do you warm to Firbank? Does it matter?
- How does this compare to modern 'escape to the country' travelogues?
- It's a personal memoir, so is the lack of Esmé's voice not actually important?

Raiders' Dawn by Alun Lewis

- What's your favourite book cover of all time?
- Should you seek pleasure instead of wisdom in libraries?
- Do pop song lyrics count as poetry?
- Why isn't Alun Lewis better known?

Poems by Lynette Roberts

- Roberts did not want her poetry reprinted – should that wish be respected?
- Should poets explain their poetry?
- Does biographical detail enrich your enjoyment of Roberts's work?
- Have you used literary podcasts to help you select your next read?

Under Milk Wood by Dylan Thomas

- Can audiobooks be better than old-fashioned paper books?
- Which films of books have you enjoyed more than the original books themselves?
- In early drafts it was titled *The Village of the Mad*, *The Town That Was Mad*, and *Llareggub: A Piece for Radio Perhaps*. How influential was the changed title on its success?
- How much does plot matter to successful fiction?

Song at the Year's Turning by R. S. Thomas
- How do you choose what to read next?
- Would somebody else's annotations put you off buying a second-hand book?
- What does Seamus Heaney mean by 'a kind of Clint Eastwood of the spirit'?
- Should Thomas have been awarded a Nobel prize?

The Awakening by Kate Roberts
- How much have things changed in Wales since Lora's day?
- If you've read any books in both the original and in translation, how did the experience compare?
- Are you more or less likely to read literature in translation?
- What might happen to Lora in a sequel?

A Toy Epic by Emyr Humphreys
- Can novellas ever be as powerful as novels?
- Does the size of the book influence how likely you are to read it?
- Which boy feels like the most fully realised character?
- Does the book try to cover too many topics?

Border Country by Raymond Williams
- How well does Will/Matthew deal with his Welsh heritage?
- Does Prosser's changing attitude to 'the workers' struggle' feel like an authentic journey?
- Would the story work better if told chronologically rather than through flashbacks?
- If you didn't know when this book was written, what date would you have guessed?

Jampot Smith by Jeremy Brooks
- Why does Brooks deliberately sets this in a real town rather than a fictional one?
- Would you be happy to be the inspiration for a character in a novel?
- Is this a war book?
- Do sex scenes ever work in literature?

Place of Stones by Ruth Janette Ruck
- Are you tempted to stay in Ruth Janette Ruck's cottage as a literary tourist?
- What is the worst book cover you've seen?
- Is it possible *not* to judge a book by its cover?
- Is the Ingrid Bergman chapter too hidden away?

One Moonlit Night by Caradog Prichard
- Do you think this is the greatest Welsh novel?
- How comfortable would you feel turning your own life into a novel?
- Is this a book about religion?
- How does the portrayal of Welsh village life compare to other books on the list?

The Small Mine by Menna Gallie
- Does Menna Gallie feel like a better novelist (*The Small Mine*) or translator (*One Moonlit Night*)?
- Does Joe Jenkins die too early in the novel? Or too late?
- Who would you cast in a film version of the book?
- Should the blurb not include such a big spoiler?

The Twelve Dancers by William Mayne

- Would you rather not know about a writer's life before reading their books?
- Should non-Welsh speakers try to reproduce spoken Welsh on the page?
- Critics often suggested Mayne's books were insufficiently gripping for children – do you think young contemporary readers would enjoy *The Twelve Dancers*?
- Which writers – for children or for adults – would you compare to Mayne?

Tide-race by Brenda Chamberlain

- Would you have been annoyed by the book if you'd been one of the islanders?
- Is this the kind of holiday destination you would enjoy?
- Could the book be described as a prose poem?
- Are you tempted to read her second island story, *The Rope of Vines*?

The Book of Three by Lloyd Alexander

- Do you ever give up on books?
- And do you ever come back to them?
- If you've seen the Disney film *The Black Cauldron*, did you realise it was based on a book?
- Does the setting feel like Wales?

The Owl Service by Alan Garner

- Do you reread books? If so, which are your favourites? If not, why not?
- To what extent is this a children's book?
- If you remember the 1969–70 television series based on the book, how does it compare?
- How important is it to have read the original story in the *Mabinogion* before reading *The Owl Service*?

The Shop in the Mountain by Showell Styles

- Should adults (re)read children's literature?
- Are blurbs useful in persuading you to buy/read books?
- Do you really need to understand mountaineering to properly appreciate this book?
- Why does Styles include Mag's supernatural experience?

Travels with a Duchess by Menna Gallie

- Would you describe this as a woman's novel?
- Is it a good title for the book?
- Why is Innes so sniffy about *How Green Was My Valley*?
- Will you be using the term 'walocs' in the future?

So Long, Hector Bebb by Ron Berry

- Would you describe this as a man's novel?
- Is boxing easier to write fiction about than other sports?
- How well does it work having so many characters relating their parts in Hector's story?
- What comparison is there between Hector and his namesake in Greek myth?

Carrie's War by Nina Bawden

- If you don't keep a list of what you've read over the last twelve months, how many can you remember now?
- Which books are you unsure if you've read?
- Why do so many children's books have supernatural elements?
- Is Carrie right – do places change more than people?

Ivor the Engine – Snowdrifts by Oliver Postgate and Peter Firmin

- Which picture books did you enjoy as a child?
- How Welsh are the *Ivor the Engine* stories?
- Do the stories work best on screen, as audio or in print?
- Why do you think the stories as a whole body of work have never been translated into Welsh?

The Volunteers by Raymond Williams

- How many times do you give an author another chance after not enjoying one of their books?
- Do you read or skip forewords and introductions to books?
- Can novels of ideas ever work as readable fiction?
- Does Redfern do the right thing?

The Sundial by Gillian Clarke

- Would you pay more for a book if it were signed or a first edition?
- What unusual annotations have you found in books you've inherited or bought second-hand?
- Poetry books generally don't sell well. Why don't people buy more?
- If there are women's novels, are there women's poetry collections, too?

On the Black Hill by Bruce Chatwin

- If this is a 'how to live your best life' exploration, are there any conclusions?
- Jünger's *On the Marble Cliffs* is a meditation on traditional values and totalitarianism – is that true of *On the Black Hill*, too?
- Is the scope of the novel too ambitious to contain within 250 pages?
- Do you agree that all unhappiness is down to our inability to stay quietly in a room?

Brothers by Bernice Rubens

- Do recent events have an impact on how you react to *Brothers*?
- Are novels that include family trees or long lists of characters overly complex?
- Is this a work of history or fiction? Or both? Or neither?
- Rubens said *Brothers* was her best book because 'what it's about matters'. What other books could you say the same about?

The Old Devils by Kingsley Amis
* What is Amis trying to do in *The Old Devils*?
* What books that are hugely successful do you think are hugely overrated?
* Why does Brydan – essentially Dylan Thomas – come in for so much criticism from Amis?
* Is this a man's book?

Work, Sex and Rugby by Lewis Davies
* Have you ever been put off a book by its title before later enjoying it?
* 'Who knows or dares to dream' is the book's epigraph – what is its significance?
* Did you find Lewis likeable?
* Does the change in narrator at the end of the book work?

Eucalyptus by Menna Elfyn
* If you don't speak/read Welsh, are you tempted to learn?
* Do poets make the best translators of poems?
* How do you read poem collections? All the way through in one go, or a bit at a time?
* Would you give away a copy of a book dedicated to you by the author?

Tree of Crows by Lewis Davies
* Why do people like reading gloomy books?
* Why has there been such a boom or renaissance in nature writing in the last few years?
* Is the book too short?
* *Tree of Crows* is often compared by critics to the works of J. G. Ballard – is that a valid assessment?

Travels in an Old Tongue by Pamela Petro
+ Which books are you surprised have found a publisher?
+ Are there degrees of Welshness? If so, what are they?
+ Do you feel a particular love for countries other than your own?
+ What is the best way to learn a language?

Five Pubs, Two Bars and a Nightclub by John Williams
+ What title would you have given this book?
+ Is this book a Welsh *Guys and Dolls*?
+ Short story collections traditionally sell badly – why do you think this is?
+ Which story would develop best into a novel?

Grits by Niall Griffiths
+ How readable did you find the novel?
+ Who is the target market for *Grits*?
+ Ianto is the main protagonist in the follow-up, *Sheepshagger*. Is he the character you would choose? If not, which character would you have chosen?
+ Almost every article written about Griffiths mentions the title widely bestowed on him of 'the Welsh Irvine Welsh' – does that feel accurate?

The Hiding Place by Trezza Azzopardi
+ Are there books, as a parent, that you find harder to read than before you had children?
+ Is 'banal bogeyman' an accurate description of Frankie? How would you describe him?
+ How successfully has Dolores pieced together her childhood?
+ How do you feel about the final scene of the book?

Aberystwyth Mon Amour by Malcolm Pryce

♦ How well does Pryce mix humour and drama?
♦ Do you need a good understanding of Welsh culture to appreciate the book?
♦ Is it fair to judge a series of books on the first one or should you read more?
♦ What are the best comedy novels you've read?

Framed by Frank Cottrell-Boyce

♦ How many Welsh artists can you name?
♦ Which of your childhood books have your children enjoyed? Or not enjoyed?
♦ Why do so many writers seem to set their stories in rural rather than urban Wales?
♦ Is the moral of the story over-egged or has Cottrell-Boyce judged it right?

Fresh Apples by Rachel Trezise

♦ Are the books you read as you get older becoming longer or shorter?
♦ Do you read short story collections from beginning to end or do you dip in randomly?
♦ Is there a constant theme linking the stories in *Fresh Apples*?
♦ How would you rearrange the order of the stories chosen by Trezise?

Running for the Hills by Horatio Clare

♦ Would you feel happy writing a memoir about your close family?
♦ How handy would you be on a farm?
♦ Can you remember your early childhood well enough to write about it in detail?
♦ Who do you feel coped better with the situation, Jenny or Robert?

Martha, Jack & Shanco by Caryl Lewis

- Is this book partly a comment on English colonialism in Wales?
- This is one of numerous shorter novels on the list – do shorter reads make for better book club choices?
- To what degree does a translated text become a co-authored one?
- Are you more likely to read a book that has won an award?

Gifted by Nikita Lalwani

- Can 'based on a true story' ever do the real life inspirations of it justice?
- Does this count as a Welsh book?
- How far should you push/encourage your children academically?
- Do you think Rumi really wanted to go to Oxford?

Resistance by Owen Sheers

- How do you feel about the pacing of the story?
- What value is there in alternate history fiction like *Resistance* and other examples such as Robert Harris's *Fatherland*, Francis Spufford's *Light Perpetual*, William Gibson's *Agency* and Philip K. Dick's *The Man in the High Castle*?
- There's another namecheck of the *Mabinogion* in *Resistance* – is there a comparable text in other literatures?
- Did you think Sarah and Albrecht would end up together?

Twenty Thousand Saints by Fflur Dafydd

- Does Bardsey sound like a good place to be a poet-in-residence?
- Who are your favourite fictional nuns?
- Until all is revealed, what did you think happened to Delyth?
- 'Wales is changing,' says the book, 'and it's important to keep up.' Is that true?

The Earth Hums in B Flat by Mari Strachan
* Do you make notes or annotations while you read?
* Can Gwenni actually fly?
* At what point did you begin to guess what had happened to Mr Evans?
* Does this feel like a debut novel?

The Meat Tree by Gwyneth Lewis
* How important is it to read the original text of the *Mabinogion* before reading *The Meat Tree*?
* Is this a feminist reworking of the *Mabinogion*?
* Are you convinced by the solution to the mystery of the spaceship?
* Nona scoffs at Campion for reading – do you think print reading will eventually die out?

The Dig by Cynan Jones
* Why do you read books?
* Have you ever stopped reading a book because of a particularly upsetting scene?
* Which dig does the title refer to?
* Is all realistic nature fiction necessarily bleak?

Pigeon by Alys Conran
* Where do you most enjoy reading?
* At what point did you guess the twist?
* How do you feel when speaking in a language that isn't your mother tongue?
* There are some graphic scenes in *Pigeon* – should books have trigger warnings?

Water Shall Refuse Them by Lucie McKnight Hardy

- Do you think Nif's parents have suspicions about what really happened to Lorry's twin sister?
- Why do you think the story is set in the Welsh borders?
- How is the heatwave relevant to the story?
- Is Nif a witch? Is Janet?

The Gododdin by Gillian Clarke

- Why does Aneirin not include any details of the battle itself?
- Would readers appreciate the book better if it were read aloud?
- Do you believe King Arthur existed?
- Why was the poem created? And why has it survived?

The Blue Book of Nebo by Manon Steffan Ros

- What is the best age to read a coming-of-age book?
- Is this a Noah's flood story for our times?
- Would you cope as well as Rowenna does in the face of a major disaster?
- Would you describe this as a crossover book?

My Family and Other Rock Stars by Tiffany Murray

- Have you ever bought a book thinking it was something completely different?
- Are comparisons between books like 'a *Hideous Kinky* for Wales' useful or pointless?
- Which of the recipes mentioned in the book would you like to try?
- Does it matter if you don't know who all the musicians in the book are?

WELSHLY BIBLIOGRAPHY

◆

All the titles in the Welshly reading list can be bought from new or second-hand booksellers at reasonable prices (or unreasonable ones if you prefer first, signed, association, etc., editions). Your local library should also be able to provide copies. As well as the publisher and the year each one was first published, I've also included details of more easily available editions if that is different.

Lloyd Alexander, *The Book of Three* (Holt, Rinehart and Winston, 1964; in the UK, Heinemann, 1966, and Usborne, 2004)

Kingsley Amis, *The Old Devils* (Hutchinson, 1986; Vintage, 2004)

Trezza Azzopardi, *The Hiding Place* (Picador, 2000)

Nina Bawden, *Carrie's War* (Victor Gollancz, 1973; Puffin Books, 1974;Virago, 2017)

Ron Berry, *So Long, Hector Bebb* (Macmillan, 1970; Parthian Library of Wales, 2006)

Jeremy Brooks, *Jampot Smith* (Hutchinson,1960; Parthian Library of Wales, 2008)

Brenda Chamberlain, *Tide-race* (Hodder & Stoughton, 1962; Seren,1987)

Bruce Chatwin, *On the Black Hill* (Jonathan Cape, 1982; Vintage, 1998)

Gillian Clarke, *The Gododdin: Lament for the Fallen* (Faber and Faber, 2021)

Gillian Clarke, *The Sundial* (Gomer Press, 1978)

Horatio Clare, *Running for the Hills: A Family Story* (John Murray, 2006)

Alys Conran, *Pigeon* (Parthian, 2016)

Frank Cottrell-Boyce, *Framed* (Macmillan, 2005)

Fflur Dafydd, *Twenty Thousand Saints* (Alcemi, 2008)

Lewis Davies, *Tree of Crows* (Parthian, 1996)

Lewis Davies, *Work, Sex and Rugby* (Parthian, 1993)

Menna Elfyn, *Eucalyptus – Detholiad o Gerddi* (Selected Poems) 1978–1994 (Gomer Press, 1995)

Thomas Firbank, *I Bought a Mountain* (George G. Harrap & Co, 1940; Short Books, 2022)

Menna Gallie, *The Small Mine* (Victor Gollancz, 1962; Honno, 2000)

Menna Gallie, *Travels with a Duchess* (Victor Gollancz, 1968; Honno, 1996 and 2011)

Alan Garner, *The Owl Service* (William Collins Sons & Co, 1967; Collins Modern Classic, 2017

Niall Griffiths, *Grits* (Jonathan Cape, 2000; Vintage, 2001)

Emyr Humphreys, *A Toy Epic* (Eyre & Spottiswoode, 1958; Seren, 1989)

Cynan Jones, *The Dig* (Granta, 2014)

David Jones, *In Parenthesis* (Faber and Faber, 1937 and 2014)

Nikita Lalwani, *Gifted* (Viking, 2007; Penguin, 2008)

Alun Lewis, *Collected Poems* (Seren, 2007)

Alun Lewis, *Raiders' Dawn* (George Allen & Unwin, 1942)

Caryl Lewis, *Martha, Jack & Shanco* (Parthian, 2007, originally published as *Martha, Jac a Sianco* by Y Lolfa, 2004)

Gwyneth Lewis, *The Meat Tree* (Seren, 2010)

Richard Llewellyn, *How Green Was My Valley* (Michael Joseph, 1939; Penguin Classics, 2001)

William Mayne, *The Twelve Dancers* (Hamish Hamilton, 1962; Puffin Books, 1964)

Lucie McKnight Hardy, *Water Shall Refuse Them* (Dead Ink, 2019)

Tiffany Murray, *My Family and Other Rock Stars* (Fleet, 2024)

Pamela Petro, *Travels in an Old Tongue: Touring the World Speaking Welsh* (HarperCollins, 1997)

Oliver Postgate and Peter Firmin, *Ivor the Engine – Snowdrifts* (Fontana Picture Lions, 1977; Severnside Books, 2006)

Caradog Prichard, *One Moonlit Night* (Canongate, 1995 and Penguin Classics, 1999, originally published as *Un Nos Ola Leuad* by Gwasg Gee, 1961)

Malcolm Pryce, *Aberystwyth Mon Amour* (Bloomsbury, 2001)

Kate Roberts, *The Awakening* (Seren, 2006; originally published as *Y Byw Sy'n Cysgu*, Gwasg Gee, 1956, and previously as *The Living Sleep*, John Jones Cardiff, 1976, and Corgi Childrens, 1981)

Lynette Roberts, *Poems* (Faber and Faber, 1944)

Lynette Roberts, *Collected Poems* (Carcanet, 2005, and scheduled to be reissued in September 2025)

Bernice Rubens, *Brothers* (Hamish Hamilton, 1983; Abacus, 1984; Penguin, 1989)

Ruth Janette Ruck, *Place of Stones* (Faber and Faber, 1961; Corgi Childrens, 1985)

Owen Sheers, *Resistance* (Faber and Faber, 2007)

Manon Steffan Ros, *The Blue Book of Nebo* (Firefly, 2022, originally published as *Llyfr Glas Nebo* by Y Lolfa, 2018)

Mari Strachan, *The Earth Hums in B Flat* (Canongate, 2009)

Showell Styles, *The Shop in the Mountain* (Victor Gollancz, 1961; Atlantic Book Publishing, 1968)

Dylan Thomas, *Under Milk Wood* (J. M. Dent, 1954; Collins Classics, 2024. Various radio, television and film recordings are available by searching online)

R. S. Thomas, *R. S. Thomas: Collected Poems: 1945–1990* (J. M. Dent, 1993)

R. S. Thomas, *Song at the Year's Turning* (Rupert Hart Davis, 1955)

Rachel Trezise, *Fresh Apples* (Parthian, 2005)

Hilda Vaughan, *The Battle to the Weak* (W. Heinemann, 1925, and Parthian Library of Wales, 2010)

John Williams, *Five Pubs, Two Bars and a Nightclub* (Bloomsbury, 1999)

Raymond Williams, *Border Country* (Chatto & Windus,1960; Hogarth Press, 1988; Parthian Library of Wales, 2005)

Raymond Williams, *The Volunteers* (Methuen, 1978; Parthian Library of Wales, 2011)

YOUR READING WELSHLY CHALLENGE

◆

Here's a space, if you choose to use it, to log your reading of Wales-related books, whether from the Welshly list or discoveries of your own. Keep going to achieve your *efydd*, *arian* and *aur* levels (bronze, silver and gold) of the Reading Welshly Challenge. Why not share your progress on social media with #MyReadingWelshly?

	TITLE	AUTHOR	DATE COMPLETED
1			
2			
3			
4			
5			
6			
7			
8			
9			

	TITLE	AUTHOR	DATE COMPLETED
10			
11			
12			

EFYDD

13			
14			
15			
16			
17			
18			
19			
20			
21			
22			
23			

	TITLE	AUTHOR	DATE COMPLETED
24			
25			

26			
27			
28			
29			
30			
31			
32			
33			
34			
35			
36			
37			

Your Reading Welshly Challenge

	TITLE	AUTHOR	DATE COMPLETED
38			
39			
40			
41			
42			
43			
44			
45			
46			
47			
48			
49			
50			
51			
52			

EXTRACTS QUOTED WITH PERMISSION FROM THE FOLLOWING COPYRIGHT HOLDERS

- Lynette Roberts, *Poems*, Carcanet Press
- R. S. Thomas, *Collected Poems: 1945–1990*, Orion Publishing Group Limited. Reproduced with permission of the Licensor through PLSclear. Copyright © R. S. Thomas 1993
- Menna Elfyn, *Eucalyptus – Detholiad o Gerddi (Selected Poems) 1978–1994*

◆

ACKNOWLEDGEMENTS

Thanks to all at Calon, especially Dr Maria Vassilopoulos for getting the ball rolling, Amy Feldman for commissioning the book, Abbie Headon for giving me a bit more time, and particularly Caleb Woodbridge who shepherded it across the line and made it a much better book with his considered comments. Also to Professor M. Wynn Thomas for his expert thoughts at an important point in the book's construction. Caroline Goldsmith is an exceptional editor and her incisive comments and suggestions have improved this book significantly. Large thanks, too, to everybody online, friends and strangers alike, who replied to my questions about Welsh writing. Menna Elfyn, Carcanet, Orion, and Angharad Rhys (on behalf of her mother Lynette Roberts) were kind enough to allow me to quote extensively from their works. A special salute to Daniel Jenkins for his generosity in sharing his library of Welshly books and recommendations as well as his infectious affection for all things Welsh.